DEAD CREATURES
TELL NO TALES

Here and there stones of some size were embedded in the gravel—or were they stones? Hosteen stopped and toed one of them over with his boot. The black eye holes of a skull stared back at him.

Hosteen found it hard to picture that great head enclosed in flesh. The angle of that fanged jaw—as long as his arm—the huge pits of eye sockets, were like nothing he had ever seen on Arzor or on fifty other planets either.

"Three eyes!" Logan's voice sounded weirdly over the lisping lap of the water. "It had three eyes!"

Also by Andre Norton
Published by Ballantine Books:

GRYPHON IN GLORY

THE JARGOON PARD

STAR GATE

THE BEAST MASTER

LORD OF THUNDER

A Del Rey Book

BALLANTINE BOOKS • NEW YORK

RLI: $\dfrac{\text{VL}: 7 + \text{up}}{\text{IL}: 6 + \text{up}}$

A Del Rey Book
Published by Ballantine Books

ISBN 0-345-31396-8

This edition published by arrangement with Harcourt Brace
Jovanovich, Inc.

Manufactured in the United States of America

First Ballantine Books Edition: February 1984

Cover art by Laurence Schwinger

ONE

Red ridges of mountains, rusted even more by the first sere breath of the Big Dry, cut across the lavender sky of Arzor north and east. At an hour past dawn, dehydrating puffs of breeze warned of the new day's scorching heat. There would be two hours—maybe three, yet—during which a man could ride, though in growing discomfort. Then he must lie up through the blistering fire of midday.

The line camp was not too far ahead. Hosteen Storm's silent communication with the powerful young stallion under him sent the horse trotting at a steady pace, striking out over a strip of range where yellow grass waved high enough to brush a rider's leg. Here and there Storm spied a moving blot of blue, the outer fringe of the grazing frawn herd. His sense of direction had not failed him when he took this short cut; they were nearing the river. In the Big Dry no animal strayed more than half a day's distance from a sure supply of water.

But he had come close to the edge of prudence in staying so long in the hills this time. One of the two canteens linked to his light saddle pad was as dry as the sun-baked rocks at his back, had been so since midmorning of the day before, and the other held no more than a good cup and a half of water. The Norbies, those wide-ranging hunters native to this frontier world, had their springs back in the mountain canyons, but their locations were clan secrets.

Perhaps here and there an off-world settler would be accepted by a clan to the point of sharing water knowledge. Logan might—Hosteen's well-marked black brows pulled in a fleeting frown as he thought of his Arzoran-born half-brother.

When Hosteen had landed on Arzor a half planet-year earlier, a veteran of the Confederacy forces after the Xik war, it was as a homeless exile. The last battle of that galaxy-wide holocaust had been a punitive raid to turn Terra into a blue, radioactive cinder. He had had no idea then that Logan Quade existed or that Brad Quade—Logan's father—could be any more to him than a man he had once sworn to kill.

In the end, the hate-twisted oath demanded of him by his grandfather on Terra had not made Storm a murderer after all. It had been broken just in time and had led him to what he needed most—new roots, a home, kin.

Only happy endings did not always remain so, Hosteen knew now. His emotion was more one of exasperation than disappointment. Though he had appeared to drop into a place already prepared to contain him as easily as his vanished Navajo kinsmen used to fit a polished turquoise into a silver setting, yet another stone in that same setting had come loose during the past few months.

To most riders, the daily round of duties on a frontier

holding were arduous enough. There were the dangerous reptilian yoris to hunt down, raiders from the wild Nitra tribe of the Peaks to keep off, a hundred and one other tangles with disaster or even sudden death to be faced. But none of that satisfied Logan. He was driven by a consuming restlessness, which pulled him away from a half-done task to seek out a Norbie camp, to join one of their wide ranging hunts, or just to wander back into the hills.

There was a flicker of black just within eye range in the sky. Hosteen's lips pursed as if for a whistle, though no sound issued from between their sun-cracked, blood-threaded surfaces. The black dot spiraled down.

The stallion halted without any outward command from his rider. With the peerless swoop of her kind, Baku, the great African Eagle, came in to settle on the pronged rest that formed the horn of Hosteen's specially designed trail saddle. The bird was panting, her head turned a little to one side as one bright and keen-sighted eye regarded Hosteen steadily.

For a long moment they sat so in perfect rapport. Science had fostered that link between man and bird, had tested and trained man, bred, tested, and trained bird, to form not just a team of two very different life forms but—when the need arose—part of a smoothly working weapon. The enemy was gone; there was no longer any need for such a weapon. And the scientists who had fashioned it had vanished into ash. But the alliance remained as steadfast here on Arzor as it had ever been on those other worlds where a sabotage and combat team of man, bird, and animals had operated with accurate efficiency.

"Nihich'i hooldoh, t'assh 'annii ya?" Hosteen asked softly, savoring the speech that perhaps he alone now along the stellar lanes would ever speak with fluency. "We're making pretty good time, aren't we?"

Baku answered with a low, throaty sound, a click of her hunter's beak in agreement. Though she relished the freedom of the sky, she wanted no more of its furnace heat in the coming day than he did. When they made the line camp, she would willingly enter its heat-dispelling cavern.

Rain, the stallion, trotted on. He was accustomed now to transporting Baku, having fitted into the animal pattern from off-world with his own contribution, speed and stamina in travel. Now he neighed shrilly. But Hosteen had already caught sight of familiar landmarks. Top that small rise, pass through a copse of muff bushes, and they were at the camp where Logan should be on duty for this ten-day period. But somehow Hosteen was already doubting he would find him there.

The camp was not a building but a cave of sorts in the side of a hillock. Following the example of native inhabitants, the settlers who ran frawns or horses in the plains set their hot weather stations deep in the cool earth. The conditioners, which controlled atmosphere for the buildings in the two small cities, the structures in the small, widely separated towns of the range country, and main houses of the holdings, were too complicated and expensive to be used in line camps.

"Halloooo." Hosteen raised his voice in the ringing hail of a camp visitor. The recessed earth-encircled doorway of the living quarters was dark. From this distance he could not tell whether it was open or closed. And the wider opening to the stable, which would give the imported horses a measure of protection, was also a blank.

But a minute later a red-yellow figure moved against the red-yellow earth at the side of the mound, and sun glinted brightly on two curves of ivory-white, breaking the natural camouflage of the waiting Norbie by revealing the six-inch horns, as normal to his domed skull as thick black hair was to Hosteen's. A long arm flashed up, and the rider recognized Gorgol, once hunter of the Shosonna tribe and now in charge of the small horse herd that was Hosteen's own personal investment in the future.

The Norbie came out of the shade of the hillock to reach for Rain's hackamore as Hosteen swung stiffly down. Brown Terran fingers flashed in fluid sign talk:

"You are here—there is trouble? Logan—?"

Gorgol was young, hardly out of boyhood, but he had already reached his full growth of limb. His six-foot, ten-inch body, all lean, taut muscle over hard, compact bone, towered over Hosteen. His yellow eyes, the vertical pupils mere threads of black against the sun's intrusive glare, did not quite meet those of the Terran, but his right hand sketched a sign for the necessity of talk.

Norbie and human vocal cords were so dissimilar as to render oral speech between off-worlder and native impossible. But the finger talk worked well between the races. An expert, as most of the range riders had to be, could express complex ideas in small, sometimes nearly invisible movements of thumb and fingers.

Hosteen went into the cave camp, Baku riding his shoulder. And while the coolness of the earth wall could only be a few degrees less than the temperature of the outside, that difference was enough to bring a sigh of content from the sweating man, a cluck of appreciation from the eagle.

9

The Terran halted inside to allow his eyes to adjust to the welcome dusk. And a single glance about told him he had guessed right. If Logan had been here, he was now gone, and not just for the early-morning duty inspection of the frawn herd. All four wall bunks were bare of sleeping rolls, there was no sign the cook unit had been used that day, and the general litter of a rider, his saddle, tote bag, and canteen, were absent.

But there was something else, a yoris hide bag, its glittering scaled exterior adorned by a feather embroidery pattern that repeated over and over the conventionalized figure of a Zamle, the flying totem of Gorgol's clan. That was the Norbie's traveling equipment—which by every right should have been stowed in a bunk locker at the Center House fifty miles downriver.

Hosteen stretched out his arm to afford Baku a bridge to the perch hammered in the wall. Then he went to the heating unit, measured out a portion of powdered "swankee," the coffee of the Arzor ranges, and dialed the pot to three-minute service. He heard the faintest whisper behind and knew that Gorgol had deliberately trodden so as to attract his attention. But he was determined to make the other give an explanation without asking any questions himself, and he knew that it was unwise to push.

While the heating unit was at work, Hosteen sailed his hat to the nearest bunk, loosened the throat lacings of his undyed frawn fabric shirt, and pulled it off before he sought the fresher and allowed water vapor to curl pleasantly and coolly about his bare chest and shoulders.

As the Terran came out of the alcove, Gorgol snapped the first swankee container out of the unit, hesitated, and drew a second, which he turned around and around in his hands, staring blank-eyed down at the liquid as if he had never seen its like before.

Hosteen seated himself on the edge of a bunk, cradled the swankee cup in his hand, and waited another long moment. Then Gorgol smacked his container down on the table top with a violence close to anger, and his fingers flew, but not with such speed that Hosteen was unable to read the signs.

"I go—there is a call for all Shosonna—Krotag summons—"

Hosteen sipped the slightly bitter but refreshing brew, his mind working faster than his deliberate movements might indicate. Why would the chief of Gorgol's clan be summoning those engaged in profitable riders' jobs? The Big Dry was neither the season for hunting nor for war—both of which pursuits, dear to the tradition and customs of the Norbies, were conducted only in the fringe months of the Wet Time. In the Big Dry, it was rigid custom for the tribes and clans to split into much smaller family groups, each to resort to one of the jealously guarded water holes to wait out the heat as best they could.

All tribes with any settler contacts strove to hire out as many of their men as riders as they could, thus removing hungry and thirsty mouths from clan supply points. To summon *in* men in the Big Dry was a policy so threatened with disaster as to appear insane. It meant trouble somewhere—bad trouble—and something that had developed in the week of Storm's own absence.

Hosteen had ridden out of the Quade Peak Holding eight days ago—to set up his square stakes and make his claim map before recording it at Galwadi. As a veteran of the forces and a Terran, he was able to file on twenty squares, and he had set out his stakes around a good piece of territory to the northeast, having river frontage and extending into the mountain foothills. There had been no whisper of trouble then, nor had he seen any signs of movement of tribes in the outback. Though, come to think of it, he had not crossed a Norbie trail or met any hunters either. That he had laid to the Big Dry. Now he wondered if more than the rigors of Arzoran seasons had wrung the natives out of the country.

"Krotag summons—in the Big Dry!" Even in finger movements one could insert a measure of incredulity.

Gorgol shifted from one yoris-hide booted foot to the other. His discomfort was plain to one who had ridden with him for months. "There is medicine talk—" His fingers shaped that and then were stiffly straight.

Hosteen sipped, his mind working fast and hard, fitting one small hint to another. "Medicine talk"—was that answer to shut off more questions or could it be the truth? In any event, it stopped him now. You did not—ever—inquire into "medicine," and his own Amerindian background made him accept that prohibition as a thing necessary and right.

"How long?"

But Gorgol's straight fingers did not immediately reply. "Not to know—" came reluctantly at last.

Hosteen was still searching for a question that was proper and yet would give him a small scrap of information when there was a clear note from the other end of the cave room, the alerting call of the com, which tied each line camp to the headquarters of the holding. The Terran went to the board, thumbing down the receive button. What came was no new message but a recall broadcast to be repeated mechanically at intervals, set to bring in all riders. There *was* something going on!

"You ride then for the hills?" he signed to Gorgol.

The Norbie was at the doorway, shouldering his travel bag. Now he paused, and not only the change of his expression showed his troubled mind. It was evident in every movement of his body. Hosteen believed the native was obeying an imperative order, greatly against his own will.

"I ride. All Norbies ride now."

All Norbies, not just Gorgol. Hosteen digested that and, in spite of himself, vented his surprise in a startled hiss. Quade depended heavily on native riders, not only here at the Peak Holding, but also down at his wider spread in the Basin. And Quade was not the only range man who had a predominance of Norbie employees. If they all took to the hills—! Yes, such an exodus could cripple some of the holdings.

"All Norbies—this, too, is medicine?"

But why? Medicine was clan business as far as Hosteen had been able to learn. He had never heard of a whole tribe or nation combining their medicine meetings and ceremonies—certainly not in the season of the Big Dry. Why, the river lands could not support such a gathering at this time of the year—let alone the arid mountain country.

But Gorgol was answering. "Yes—all Norbies." quivers—that was unheard of!

"Also the wild ones?"

"The wild ones—yes."

Impossible! There were tribal feuds nursed for the

13

honor of fighting men. To send in the peace pole for a clan, or perhaps—stretching it far—several clans at a time, was one thing. But for the Shosonna and the Nitra to sit under such a pole with their war arrows still in the the quivers—that was unheard of!

"I go—" Gorgol slapped his travel bag. "The horses, they are in the big corral—you will find them safe."

"You go—but you will return to ride again?" Hosteen was bothered by the suggestion of finality in the other's signs.

"That lies with the lightning—"

The Norbie was gone. Hosteen walked back across the room to lie down on a bunk. So Gorgol was not even sure he would be back. What did he mean about that lying with the lightning? The Norbies recognized divine power in shadow beings who drummed thunder and used the lightning to slay. The reputed home of these God Ones was the high mountains of the northeast. And those same mountains also hid the caverns and passages of that mysterious unknown race who had either explored or settled here on Arzor centuries before the Terran exploration ships had reached this part of the galaxy.

Hosteen, Logan, and Gorgol, together with Surra, the dune cat, and Hing, the meercat of the Beast Team, had discovered the Cavern of the Hundred Gardens, a fabulous botanical preserve of the Sealed Caves. That, and the ruined city or fortification in the valley beyond, was still under scientific study. It was easy to believe that there were other Sealed Caves in the hills—and also easy to understand that the Norbies had made gods of the long-vanished and still-unknown space travelers who had hollowed out the Peaks to hold their mysteries.

Hosteen could spend hours speculating about that and not turn up one real fact. Now it was better to sleep through the day heat and ride out at night to answer the return order from the holding. For all Hosteen knew, that summons might have been sounding for days, which could account for Logan's absence. He turned on his side and willed himself to sleep.

That mental alarm clock that had been conditioned into him during his service days brought him awake hours later. To come out of the cave into the dusk of evening was walking into a wall of heavy heat, but it was not as bad as sunlight. He allowed Rain to splash in the shallows of the river before he swung up to the riding pad. Baku's world was not that of the night, but she accepted it at his urging, climbing into the star-encrusted sky.

The Center House was three nights' ride from the line camp. And two of the days in between Hosteen had to spend in improvished shelters, lying flat on the earth to get what coolness the parched soil might provide. Shortly before midnight on the third night, he rode up to the blazing light of his goal. The unusual glare of atom lamps was another warning of emergency.

"Who's there?" The suspicion-sharp hail out of the gate shadows made the Terran draw rein. Then from his right a furry body materialized beside the snorting stallion, reared on its haunches, and drew a paw with sheathed claws along Hosteen's boot.

"Storm," he answered the challenger and dismounted to caress Surra. The rasp of the dune cat's tongue on his hand was an unusually fervid greeting, which awoke answering warmth within him.

"I'll take your horse." The man who came from the

gate carried an unholstered stunner. "Quade's been wait-in', hopin' you'd make it soon—"

Hosteen muttered a brief thanks, more interested in the fact that there were other men in the courtyard. But there were no Norbies, not a single one of the native riders he was used to seeing there. Gorgol had been right; the Norbies had all pulled out.

With Surra rubbing against his thigh, now and then butting him playfully with her head, he went to the door of the big house. Tension was alive in the cat, too. She had sometimes been like this on the eve of one of their wartime forays. Trouble excited but did not worry Surra.

"—continent-wide as far as reports have come in—"

Maybe Surra was exhilarated by the present happenings, but the tone of that voice told Hosteen that Brad Quade was frankly worried.

TWO

Within the house, Hosteen found himself fronting a distinguished gathering that included most of the settlers in the Peak country—even Rig Dumaroy, whose usual association with Brad Quade was one of uneasy neutrality. But, of course, in any Norbie trouble Dumaroy would be present. He was the one large holder in the frontier country who was prejudiced against the Arzoran natives and refused to hire any of them.

"It's Storm—" Dort Lancin, who had ridden in with the Terran on the military transport almost a year ago, waved two fingers in greeting, a sign that was also a hunter signal for watchfulness.

The tall man standing by the com board glanced over his shoulder, and Hosteen read a shadow of relief on his stepfather's face.

Dort Lancin, his older and more taciturn brother Artur, Dumaroy, Jotter Hyke, Val Palasco, Connar Jaffe, Sim Starle—but no Logan Quade. Hosteen stood inside the doorway, his hand resting on Surra's head as the big cat nuzzled against his legs.

"What's going on?" he asked.

Dumaroy, a wide and rather vindictive grin on his face, answered first.

"All your pet goats have lit out for the hills. Always said they'd cross you up, always said it—now you see. And I say"—his grin faded, and he brought his big hand down on his knee in a resounding slap—"there's trouble brewing up there. The sooner we fort up and send for the Patrol to come in and settle this once and for all—"

Artur Lancin's level voice, threaded with weariness, cut across the other's bellow with the neatness of a belt knife slicing through frawn fat. "Yes, you've been broadcastin' on that beam all night, Dumaroy. We received you loud and clear the first time. Storm," he addressed the younger man, "you see anything different out in the hills?"

Storm flipped his hat up on the daryork horn rack and unfastened the belt that supported his stunner and bush knife as he replied.

"I think now what I did *not* see is important."

"That being?" Brad Quade was pulling a fresh swankee container from the unit. He brought it over and then, with a fingertip touch on Hosteen's shoulder, guided him to a foam chair.

"No hunters—no trails—nothing." Hosteen sipped the restoring liquid between words. He had not realized how bone-aching tired he was until he sat down. "I might have been riding in an empty world—"

The two Lancins watched him narrowly, and Dort nodded. He had hunted with the Norbies, was welcome in their villages, and well understood the strangeness of an empty country.

"How far did you go?" Quade asked.

"I made the rounds to set up markers." Hosteen brought his claim map from the inner pocket of his shirt. Quade took the sheet from him and compared its lines with the country survey chart that was a mural for one wall of the room.

"Clean up to the gorge, eh?" Jaffe commented. "And no hunter sign?"

"No. I thought it was because of the Big Dry retreat—"

"That wouldn't come quite this early," Quade replied. "Gorgol brought in your cavvy of mounts four days ago, took his bag, and rode off."

"I met him at the line camp."

"What did he tell you?"

"That there was a clan summons out—some sort of intertribal gathering—"

"Durin' the Big Dry?" demanded Hyke incredulously.

"I told you!" Dumaroy pounded with his fist this time, and Hosteen heard a snarling rumble from Surra. He sent a mental command to silence the cat. "I told you! We're sittin' right here on the only free runnin' water that keeps on runnin' through the worst of the Dry. And those goats are gonna come down and try to butt us out of it! If we've the sense of water rats, we'll go up and clean 'em out before they can get organized—"

"Once before you moved up to clean out Norbies," Quade said coldly. "And what did we find out—that the Norbies weren't responsible for anything that had happened—that there was an Xik holdout group behind all our stock losses!"

"Yeah—and is this another Xik trick? Callin' in all the tribes now?" Dumaroy's hostility was like a fog spreading from him toward the other man.

"Maybe not Xik this time," Quade conceded. "But I refuse to make any move until I know more about the situation. All we are sure of at present is that our Norbie riders have quit and are heading for the mountains at a time when they are usually eager to work, and that this has not happened before."

Artur Lancin stood up. "That's sense, Dumaroy. We aren't goin' to stick our heads into some yoris' mouth just on your say-so. I say we do a little scoutin'. Meanwhile, we rustle up riders from the Basin or even pick up some drifters from the Port to tide us over. With the Dry on, the herds aren't goin' to move too far from the river, and we'll need only a yoris patrol and some count work. My granddad got through, ridin' on his own, with just his two boys to back him in the First Ship days. None of you here look too soft for the saddle now."

"That's right," Sim Starle agreed. "We'll keep our coms on a circle hookup and with the alert on. Anybody learns anything, he sends the word out on the beam. I'm for sittin' quiet until we're sure about what's happenin' and why. Maybe these Norbies are havin' them a medicine powwow—and that's none of our danged business!"

Hosteen, sinking deeper into his fog of weariness, watched the settlers leave for their 'copters, to fly back to the scattered holdings of the Peak country. He was still too torpid to move when Brad Quade re-entered, having seen off the company. But he roused himself to ask the one question bothering him most.

"Where's Logan?"

"Gone—"

The tone of the other's voice pulled Hosteen out of his lethargy of fatigue. "Gone! Where?"

"To Krotag's camp—at least that's what I think—"

Hosteen was on his feet now. "The young fool! This is medicine business, Gorgol said so—"

Brad Quade turned. His face might seem impassive to an outsider, but it did not hide his feelings from Hosteen. "I know. But he has drunk blood with Kavok, Krotag's first son. That makes him a clansman—"

Hosteen bit back his protest. "Medicine" was tricky. A man could be an adopted clansman, living in blood brotherhood with a Norbie, but that might not cover prying into the inner beliefs of the natives. There was no use putting his thoughts and fears into words. Brad Quade knew all that and more.

"I can make it back up to the washes. How much of a start has he?"

"No. This was his choice; he took it with his eyes open. You won't ride after him. Tomorrow, if you will, I want you on the way to Galwadi in the 'copter."

"Galwadi!"

Brad Quade picked up the claim map. "You have this to record, remember? Then—have a talk with Kelson. He knows Logan." Quade ran one hand through his thick black cap of wiry hair. "I wish Kelson had got that bill through the Council—Logan was so keen on that Ranger business they talked about. If that had gone through, maybe he'd have had a job he'd really settle down to. But you can't make the Council hump just the way you want them to—even when you prod. Anyway—you see Kelson and try to get a line on what's happening. There may have been an official clamp on Norbie news—I suspect that. And I'd better stay here for now. Dumaroy's just hotheaded enough to try one of those dangerous schemes of his if there's no one to talk him down—and just one incident might set off big trouble."

"What do *you* think is happening?"

Brad Quade hooked his thumbs in his wide rider's belt and stared at the floor as if he had never seen such a pattern of river stones before. "I have no idea. This is 'medicine' right enough—but it's unique at this time of the year. The Quades were First Ship people. I've found nothing in our family records like this—"

"Gorgol told me the peace poles were up for the wild tribes."

His stepfather nodded. "I know; he told me, too. But just to sit and wait—"

Hosteen made one of his rare gestures of feeling toward this man he had once sworn to kill, resting a brown hand on the other's wide shoulder.

"To wait is always the hardest. Tomorrow night I will go to Galwadi. Logan—he is Norbie under the skin, and he has drunk blood with the Zamle Shosonna. That is a sacred thing—big medicine—"

Brad Quade's hand came up to cover Hosteen's for a moment of shared warmth. "Big enough—we can hope that. Now, you look like a two-day marcher in the flats. Get to bed and rest!"

To wait—Hosteen felt the first pinch of his own private kind of waiting as he sat in the 'copter boring through the night sky on the way to Galwadi. Behind him he left everything that counted on Arzor—a soft-furred, keen-eyed cat with a coat of yellow and a brain that perhaps matched his own in intelligence, though that intelligence might be of a different order, a horse he had trained, Hing, the meercat, a small, tumbling, clownish animal that had waddled four half-grown kits out for his inspection earlier that very evening, Baku, perched on the top corral bar, bidding him farewell with a falcon scream. And a man, a man whom he had once respected even while he hated him and whom he would now follow anywhere, anytime, and for any purpose. He left all those in what might be the heart of enemy territory if their forebodings crystallized into the worst of futures.

To all outward seeming, there was no tension in Galwadi. Hosteen, coming from the land registration office, eyed the traffic on the street speculatively. The hour was far into dusk, and the small city, which had been dead in the day's heat, was alive now, the streets and shops busy. But whether he could hire any riders here was another question. To get new light-and-tie men at this season was a problem. There were several gather-ins in the lower town, and those would be a starting place for his quest. But first—dinner.

He chose a small, quiet eating place and was surprised at the wide array of dish dials he was offered. Food on the holdings was usually plentiful but plain, with little variety. The few off-world luxury items were carefully saved for holidays. But here he was fronted with a choice such as was more usual in a Port city catering to off-world visitors. Then he noted a Zacathan in the next booth and realized that a restaurant in the capital needs must satisfy the alien government representatives as well as the settlers.

Deciding to plunge, Hosteen dialed three dishes he had not tasted since his last service leave. He was sipping at a tube planted in a dalee bulb when someone paused by his table, and he glanced up to see Kelson, the Peace Officer of the Peak section.

"Heard you were looking for me, Storm."

"Tried your office com," Hosteen assented. He was a little at a loss as to how to word his question. Should he just bluntly ask what was up—if there was any news being withheld from the holdings? But Kelson continued.

"Coincidence. I was trying to reach you. Called the Peaks—Quade said you were here registering your squares. You've decided to settle in the Peak country then?"

"Yes—horse breeding with Put Larkin. He's off-world now. Heard of a new crossbreed on Astra—Terran blood interbred with the local species of duicorn. Can stand up to desert heat there—or so the breeder claims."

"So they might do for the Big Dry here, eh? It's a thought. But your range isn't open yet—"

What did that matter, Hosteen wondered. No one would start on holding work until the rains came. But Kelson was beckoning to someone across the room.

"There's a problem—maybe you can help us," the Peace Officer continued. "Mind if we join you? Time's essential in this one—"

The man who came up was an off-worlder of a type usually not seen on a frontier world. His sleek form-fitting tunic, picked out with a silver-thread pattern, and the long hose-breeches of flat black were those of a business executive on one of the densely populated merchant worlds, and fashionable though they might have been on his home planet, they were as incongruous here as they were ill-becoming to his pudgy figure. Ridiculous as he might look in this Arzoran restaurant, one did not think him a figure of fun when one observed his craggy face, saw the square set of a determined and forceful chin and the bleak eyes that were those of a man used to giving orders. Hosteen recognized the breed and stiffened—it was one with which he had little sympathy.

"Gentle Homo Lass Widders, Beast Master Storm." Kelson made the introductions, using the title of respect from the inner planets for the stranger, who seated himself without invitation across the table from Hosteen and proceeded to survey the Terran with an appraisal the other found insolent.

"I am not of the forces now." Hosteen corrected Kelson perversely. "So it is not Beast Master—today I light and tie for Quade."

"You're a holding head rather since an hour ago, aren't you? You've located your stakes. Have you set up a brand?" Kelson asked.

"Arrowhead S," Storm replied absently. "And what do you wish of a mustered-out Beast Master, Gentle Homo?"

"About a month, maybe more, of your time and services," Widders rapped out in the clicking Galactic basic of the business worlds. "I want to have you—and your team—guide me into the Blue section—"

Hosteen blinked and looked to Kelson for confirmation that he had really heard that idiotic statement. To his surprise, the expression on the Peace Officer's face read that this stranger from one of the hothouse worlds meant exactly what he said.

"It is a matter of time, Beast Master. I understand we must get into that country within the next two weeks if we go at all before next season."

Hosteen did not blink this time. He merely replied with the truth.

"Impossible."

"Nothing," returned Widders with his irritating confidence, "is impossible, given the right man and credits enough. Kelson believes you are the man, and I can provide the credits."

There was no use giving this madman a blanket denial; he would not accept that. Listen to his story, get the reason behind this insane plan, then prove to him its utter folly—that was the only way to proceed.

"Why the Blue?" Hosteen asked as he spooned up some lorg sauce and spread it neatly over a horva fritter.

"Because my son's there—"

Again Hosteen glanced at Kelson. The Blue was unknown. Those mountains, which were its western ramparts, were known, and appeared on the maps of the Peak country. But what lay behind that barrier existed only as a series of hazy aerial photos. The treacherous air currents of those heights had kept out 'copter surveys, and the territory was the hunting ground of the feared wild Norbie cannibals, hated, shunned, and fought by their own kind of generations. No one—government man, settler, yoris hunter—had ever gone into the Blue and returned. It was posted off limits by government order. Yet here was Kelson listening to a proposal to invade the forbidden section as if Widders was doing no more than suggesting a stroll down a Galwadi street. Again Hosteen waited for enlightenment.

"You're a veteran of Confed forces, Storm. Well, my son is, too. He served with a Breakaway Task Force—"

Hosteen was a little jarred. To find an inner planet man among the Breakaways—those tough, very tough, first-in-fighters—was unusual.

"He was wounded, badly, just before the Xik collapse. Since then he has been on Allpeace—"

Allpeace, one of the rehabilitation worlds where men were rebuilt from human wreckage to live passably normal lives again. But if young Widders had been on Allpeace, how had he gotten into the Blue on Arzor?

"Eight months ago a transport left Allpeace with a hundred discharged veterans on board, Iton among them. On the fringe of this system, that ship hit a derelict hyper bomb." Widders might have been discussing the weather if you did not watch his eyes and note that small twitch of lip he could not control.

"Just a month ago a lifeboat from that ship was discovered on Mayho, this planet's sister world. There were two survivors. They reported that at least one more LB left the transport, and they cruised with her into this system. Their boat was damaged, and they had to set down on Mayho. Their companion headed on here to Arzor, promising to send back help—"

"And didn't arrive," Hosteen stated instead of questioned.

But Kelson was shaking his head. "No—there is a chance she did arrive, that she crashed in the Blue. Weak signals of some sort were recorded on robot coms in two

27

different line camps out in the Peaks. A cross check gives us a Blue landing point."

"And your local climate would mean death to any survivors out there without adequate supplies or transportation at this season," Widders continued. "I want you to guide me in—to get my son out—"

If he *was* on that LB and is still alive, Hosteen added silently. But he made his oral reply as plain as he could.

"You are asking the impossible, Gentle Homo. To go into the Blue at this time is simply suicide, and there is no possible way of getting behind the Peaks during the Big Dry."

"Natives live there all year around, don't they?" Widders' voice scaled up a note or two.

"Yes, the Norbies live there. But their knowledge of the country is not shared with us."

"You can hire native guides, anything you need. There is no limit on funds—"

"Credits can't buy water knowledge from a Norbie. And there is also this—right now the tribes are making medicine in the Peak country. We would not be able to ride in under those conditions even in the Wet Time when all the odds are in our favor."

"I've heard about that," Kelson said. "It has to be looked into—"

"Not by me!" Hosteen shook his head. "There's trouble shaping up back there. I'm down here partly to report it and to try and hire riders to replace our Norbies. Every native has pulled out of the Peak country during the past week—every one—"

Kelson did not appear surprised. "So we heard. And they are moving northeast."

"Into the Blue." Hosteen digested that.

"Just so. You were a short way into that country when you discovered that Xik nest. And Logan—he's hunted along there. You're the only two settlers who have any ground-level information we can use," Kelson added.

"No." Hosteen tried to make that negative sound final. "I'm not completely crazy. Sorry, Gentle Homo, the Blue is closed country—in more ways than one."

Widders' eyes were no longer bleak. There was a spark of anger in their gray depths. "If I refuse to accept that?"

Hosteen slipped a credit disk into the table slot. "That is your privilege, Gentle Homo, and none of my business. See you later, Kelson." He rose and walked away from Widders and his problems. He had his own to deal with now.

THREE

"That's it—" For some reason Storm could not sit still but strode up and down the length of the big main room of the holding while he gave the results of his mission to Galwadi. "I hired just one rider, and I had to bail him out of Confinement—"

"What had he done?" Brad Quade asked.

"Tried to wipe off the pavement of a street, using the aeropilot of the Valodian minister for a mop. The minister was rather upset about it—his protests got Havers twenty days or forty credits. He'd lost his last credit at Star and Comet, so he was sweating out the twenty days. Had served three of them when I paid his fine. He seems to know his business, though."

"And you saw Kelson?"

"Kelson saw me. He's blown all his rockets and is spinning in for a big smash if you ask me." Unconsciously Storm dropped into the old service slang.

There was a soft growl from the shadows, where Surra

picked up his mood of irritation and faint apprehension, translating it into her own form of protest.

"What did he say?"

"He had an inner-planet civ in tow. They wanted a guide into the Blue—right now!"

"What?" Quade's incredulity was as great as Hosteen's own had been back in Galwadi.

Swiftly he outlined Widders' story.

"That could all be true, though why he's so sure his son was on board that LB—wish-thinking, I suppose." Quade shook his head. "A Norbie might just make it. Only you're not going to find a Norbie who will try, now now. On the other hand—" Quade's voice trailed off. He was sitting quietly at his file desk, two of Hing's kits curled up in his lap, a third cuddled down on his shoulder. Now he looked to the map on the wall. "On the other hand, that might be just the direction in which we should do some prospecting."

"Why?"

"Dort Lancin made a swing up the valley in his 'copter. He spotted two clans on the march, and they weren't just shifting camp. They were moving with a purpose—so fast they had left a stray mare—"

Storm stopped pacing, eying his stepfather with startled interest. For a Norbie to abandon a horse under any circumstances, except to save life, was so unheard of as to join in magnitude Widders' desire to enter the Blue.

"Heading northeast?" He was not the least surprised to be answered by a nod.

"I can't understand it. That's worse than Nitra country—that's where they eat THE MEAT." He made the Arzoran sign for the cannibal tribes. "No Shosonna or

31

Warpt or Fanga would head in that direction. He'd be ritually unclean for years—"

"Just so. But that's where they're going—not raiding parties but the clans, with their women and children. So I agree this much with Kelson—we ought to know what is going on back there. But how any of us could get in—that is a different matter."

Storm went to the map. " 'Copter would crack up if those wind currents are all they're reported to be."

"They are, all right," Quade returned with grim emphasis. "You might—with a crack pilot—do some exploring along the fringe under the right conditions and weather. But you couldn't make any long survey flight into that region. Any exploring party would have to go on horses or afoot."

"The Norbies do have wells—"

"Which are clan secrets and not shared with us."

Storm was still tracing the lines of the mountains on the mural map. "Did Logan ever learn any well calls?"

Though the human voice box could not duplicate Norbie speech, nor a Norbie produce anything like a Galactic basic word, there was a rarer form of communication that some of the Arzor-born settlers—those initiated deeply enough into native ways—could understand, even if they could not imitate it themselves. Long, lilting calls, which were almost like songs, were a known code. These were used by native scouts as warnings or reports, and it was common knowledge among the riders that some were used only to signal the appearance or disappearance of water.

"He might have."

"You're sure he is riding with Krotag?"

"He wouldn't be allowed to join any other clan."

The meercats awoke, squeaked. Again Surra growled, alert to the tension behind that quiet answer. Then the big cat padded soft-footed to the door.

"Someone's coming—" Storm stated the obvious. Surra was familiar with every living thing at the holding, human, animal, Norbie. She was waiting now for a stranger.

The dune cat's phenomenal hearing and her better than human nose had heralded the newcomers long before they reached the door, where Quade now stood in the cool gloom of very early morning to welcome them. A path of light from the window picked out the green tunic of a Peace Officer, and a moment later the visitor's hail came in Kelson's voice.

"Hallo—the holding!"

"The fire is waiting!" Brad Quade called back the customary answer.

Storm was not in the least surprised to see that Kelson's companion was Widders, who, in his finicky civ dress, looked even more out of place in the comfortable but rather rough-hewn main chamber. Its chief decorations were trophies of Norbie weapons on the walls, its heavy furnishings were made out of native wood by settler hands, and a few off-world mementos of Brad Quade's roving past as an officer of Survey were scattered around.

Widders crossed the threshold with an authoritative stride and then halted quickly as he fronted Surra. The big cat regarded him with a long, wide-eyed stare. Storm knew that she had not only imprinted the civ's appearance on her memory for all time but had also made up her mind concerning him, and that her opinion was not in any way flattering to the off-world Gentle Homo. Majestically, she moved to the far side of the room and leaped to the low couch, which was her own particular seat. But she did not curl up at ease; instead she sat upright, the nervous tip of her fluffy fox tail just brushing her foretoes, her vulpine ears at attention.

Storm busied himself at the heating unit to produce the inevitable cups of swankee. His early tension was increased now. Kelson had brought Widders here. That meant that neither the off-worlder nor the officer had given up the wild scheme about the Blue, but Quade's word would carry weight. Hosteen did not believe that the others were going to be satisfied with the outcome of the interview.

"Glad you came," Quade said to Kelson. "We've a problem here—"

"I have a problem, Gentle Homo," Widders cut in. "I understand you have a son who knows the outback regions very well, has hunted over them. I'd like to see him—as soon as possible—"

Quade's face showed no signs of a frown, but just as Hosteen knew Surra's emotions, he was aware of the flick of temper that brash beginning aroused in Brad Quade.

"I have two sons," the settler replied deliberately, "both of whom can claim a rather extensive knowledge of the Peaks. Hosteen has already told me of your wish to enter the Blue."

"And he has refused to try it." Widders was smoldering under his shell. He was not a man used to, or able to accept, opposition.

"If he had agreed, he would need remedial attention from a conditioner," Quade returned dryly. "Kelson, you know the utter folly of such a plan."

The Peace Officer was staring into the container of swankee he held. "Yes, I know all the risks, Brad. But we have to get in there—it's imperative! And chiefs such as Krotag will accept a mission like this as an excuse—they can understand a father in search of his son."

So that was it—a big piece of puzzle slipped neatly into place. Hosteen began to realize that Kelson was making sense after all. There was a reason for exploring the Blue, an imperative reason. And Widders' quest would be understandable to the Norbies, among whom family and clan ties were close. A father in search of his missing son—yes, that could be a talking point, which normally would gain Widders native guides, mounts, maybe even the use of some of the hidden water sources. But the important word in that was "normally." This was not a normal Big Dry, and the clans were acting very abnormally.

"Logan has blood drink-brothers or a brother with Krotag's clan, hasn't he?" Kelson pushed on. "And you"—he looked to Hosteen—"are a hunt and war companion of Gorgol."

"Gorgol's gone."

"And so has Logan," Quade added. "He rode off five days ago to join Krotag's drift—"

"Into the Blue!" Kelson exclaimed.

"I don't know."

"The Zamle clan were in the First Finger." Kelson put down his drink and went to the wall map. "They were in camp here last time I checked." He stabbed a forefinger on one of the long, narrow canyons striking up into the Peaks, almost a roadway into the Blue.

Storm moved uneasily, picked up a wandering meercat kit, and held it cupped against his chest, where it patted him with small forepaws and chittered drowsily. Logan had gone with the clan. The reasons for doing it might matter, but the fact that he had gone mattered more. The boy might be condemned by his own recklessness, facing more than just the perils of the Big Dry.

Continuing to stare at the map without really seeing its configurations, Hosteen began to plan. Rain—no, he could not ride Rain. The stallion was an off-world import without even one year's seasoning here. He'd need native-bred mounts—two at least, though four would be better. A man had to keep changing horses in the Big Dry. He'd need two pack animals per man for water transport. Other supplies would necessarily be concentrates that did not satisfy a body used to normal food but which provided the necessary energy to keep men going for days.

Surra? Hosteen's head turned ever so slightly; he linked to the cat in inental contact. Yes—Surra. There was an answering thrust of eagerness that met his wordless question. Surra—Baku—Hing had her maternal duties here, and there would be no need for her particular talents as a saboteur. With Baku and Surra, maybe no chance became a small chance. Their senses, so much keener than any human's or Norbie's, might locate those needful wells in the outback.

Now Quade broke the short silence with a question, deferring to his stepson with the respect for the other's training and ability he had always shown. "A chance?"

"I don't know—" Storm refused to be hurried. "Seasoned mounts, concentrates, water transport—"

"Supplies can be flown in by 'copter!" Widders pounced at the hint of possible victory.

"You'll have to have an experienced pilot, a fine

machine, and even then you dare not go too far into those heights," Quade declared. "The air currents are crazy back there—"

"Dumps stationed along the line of march." Kelson's voice held a note almost as eager as Widders'. "We could plant those by 'copter—water, supplies—all the way through the foothills."

The idea became less impossible as each man visualized the possibilities of using off-world transportation in part. Yes, supply dumps could nurse an expedition along to the last barrier walling off the Blue, providing there was no hostile reaction from the Norbies. But beyond that barrier, much would depend upon the nature of the territory the heights guarded.

"How soon can you start?" Widders demanded. "I can have supplies, an expert pilot, a 'copter ready to go in a day."

Again the antagonism Hosteen had felt at their first meeting awoke in the younger man.

"I have not yet decided whether I shall go," he replied coldly. " 'Asizi," he said, giving Quade the title of Navajo chieftainship and slipping into the common tongue of the Amerindian Tribal Council, "do you think this thing can be done?"

"With the favor of the Above Ones and the fortune of good medicine, there is a chance of success for a warrior. That is my true word—over the pipe," Quade answered in the same language.

"There is this." In basic, Storm again addressed both Widders and Kelson. "Let it be understood that I am undertaking this expecting trouble. On the trail, the decision is mine when there comes a time to say go forward or retreat."

Widders frowned and plucked at a pouted lower lip with thumb and forefinger. "You mean, you are to be in absolute command—to have all the right of judgment?"

"That is correct. It is my life I risk, and those of my team. Long ago I learned the folly of charging against too high odds. The decisions must be mine."

A hot glance from those coals that lay banked behind Widders' eyes told him of the civ's resentment.

"How many men do you want?" Kelson asked. "I can spare you two, maybe three from the Corps."

Storm shook his head. "Me alone, with Surra and Baku. I shall strike up the First Finger and try to locate Krotag's clan. With Logan—and Gorgol, if I am able to persuade him to join us—there will be enough. A small party, traveling light, that is the only way."

"But I am going!" Widders flared.

Hosteen answered that crisply. "You are off-world, not only off-world but not even trail-trained. I go *my* way or not at all!"

For a second or so it seemed that Widders would hold stubbornly to his determination to make one of the party. Then he shrugged when glances at Kelson and Quade told him they believed Hosteen was right.

"Well—how soon?"

"I must select range stock, make other preparations—two days—"

"Two days!" Widders snorted. "Very well. I am forced to accept your decision."

But Storm was no longer aware of him. Surra had flowed past the men to the door, and the urgency she broadcast brought the Beast Master after her. Dawn was just firing the sky but had not lit the mountains to a point where man and cat could not see that burst. Very far away, just on the rim of the world, a jaffered sword thrust up into the heavens. Lightning—but it was out of season for lightning, and those flashes descended and did not pierce skyward as these had done. They were gone before Storm could be certain he had seen anything of consequence.

Surra snarled, spat. Then Hosteen caught it, too, not truly sound but a vibration in the air, so distant and faint as to puzzle a man as to its actual existence. Back in the Peaks something had happened.

The scream of an aroused and belligerent eagle deadened the small sounds of early morning. From her perch by the corral, Baku gave forth another war cry that was answered by the trumpeting of Rain, the squeals of other herd stallions, the neighing of mares. Whatever the vibration had been, it had reached the animals, aroused in them quick and violent reaction.

"What is it?" Quade came out behind Storm, followed by Kelson, less speedily by Widders.

"I think 'anna 'Hwii'iidzii," Storm found himself saying in Navajo without really knowing why, "a declaration of war, 'Asizi."

"And Logan's back there!" Quade stared at the Peaks. "That settles it—I ride with you."

"Not so, 'Asizi. It is as you have said before. This country is ripe for trouble. You alone perhaps can hold the peace. I take with me Baku. If there is a need, she can come back for you and others. Logan, more than any of us, is friend to the clans. And the blood-drink bond is binding past even a green-arrow feud."

He watched Quade anxiously. It was not in him to boast of his own qualifications, but he knew that his training and the control of the team gave him an advantage no other man now in the river valley had. Quade knew Arzor, he had hunted in the Peaks, but Quade and Quade alone could keep the settlers in line. To be caught between whatever danger lay in the Blue and a punitive posse headed by Dumaroy was an additional peril Storm had no mind to face. He had had a taste of Dumaroy's hotheaded bungling of a similar situation months earlier when the Xik holdout post had been the object of the settlers' attack.

Somehow Brad Quade summoned a ghost of a smile. "There is that in you which I trust, at least in this matter. Also—perhaps Logan will listen to hanaai, the elder brother, where he closes his ears to hataa, his father. Why this should be—" He was talking to himself now.

The horses were quieting, and the men went back to the house, where they consulted maps, located dump sites. At last Kelson and Widders bedded down for the day heat before flying back to Galwadi to set up the supply lift. Hosteen lay down wearily on his own bed only to discover that he could not sleep, tired as he was.

That flash in the Peaks, the ghost of sound or air disturbance that had followed it—he could not believe they were signs of some phenomenal weather disturbance. Yet what else could they be?

" 'Anaasazi"—the ancient enemy ones," he whispered.

Half a year ago, he, Gorgol, and Logan had found the Cavern of the Hundred Gardens, where the botanical treasures of as many different worlds grew luxuriantly and unwithered, untouched by time, just as the unknown aliens had left them in the hollow shell of a mountain ages earlier. There had been nothing horrible or repelling about those remains of the unknown civilization of space rovers. In fact, the gardens had been welcoming, enchanting, giving men healing and peace. And because of the gardens, the aliens had since been considered benevolent, though no further such finds had been made.

Archaeologists and Survey men had picked into the roundabout mountains, tried to learn something more from the valley of ruins beside the garden mountain—to no avail so far. However, one mountain had hidden beauty and delight, so more mountains might contain their own secrets. And the mountains of the Blue were the essence of the unknown. That strange premonition of danger that had awakened in Storm at the sight and sound of the early morning could not be eased. He was somehow very certain his goal was not a fanciful garden this time.

FOUR

Yesterday Hosteen had reached the first of the dumps, strategically located where a crevice gave him and his animals cover during the day. But he was not making the time he had hoped. In this broken country, even with Surra's keen eyesight and the horses' instinct to rely upon, he dared not travel too fast at night, and the early morning hours, those of the short dusk, were too few.

But so far, he had had tracks to follow. Trails left by the Norbies crossed and recrossed, made by more than one clan, until in some places he discovered a regular roadway. And he found indications that backed Dort Lancin's initial report—the natives were pushing onward at a pace that was perilous in this season. One could almost believe they were being herded on into the hills by some relentless pursuer or pursuers.

There had been no recurrence of the phenomenon in the Peaks, and neither Surra nor Baku had given Storm any more than routine warnings. Yet the vague uneasiness was with Hosteen still as he picked his way along the dried stream bed that bottomed this gorge, his horses strung out with drooping heads.

An alert came from Surra. With a jerk of the lead rein, Hosteen brought the horses against the cliff wall and waited for another message from his furred scout before taking cover himself. Then he heard a trill, rising and falling like the breathy winds of the Wet Time. It was a Norbie signal—and, the Terran hoped. Shosonna. But his stunner was now in his hand to serve if he were wrong.

There—Surra had relaxed. The sentry or scout ahead was not a stranger to her. Hosteen believed that the native had not sighted the dune cat. Her fur was so close in color to the ground that she could be invisible if she wished it so.

Hosteen plodded forward once more, leading his horses, not wanting to ride in the thick heat until he had to. One more hour, maybe less, and he must hole up for the day. But, at a second alert from his feline scout, he swung up on the saddle pad. There was a dignity to be maintained between Norbie and outlander, and mounted man faced mounted native in equality, especially when there might be a point of bargaining ahead.

The Terran called. His voice echoed hollowly back from canyon walls, magnified and distorted until it could have been the united shout of a whole party. One of the wiry black-and-white-coated range horses from a Norbie cavvy came into view, and on it sat Gorgol. The Norbie rider did not advance. His face was expressionless. They might have been strangers meeting trailwise for the first time. Nor did the native's hands loose the reins preparatory to making finger talk. It was Hosteen who gave the first hand gesture.

43

"I seek Logan—this is a matter not to be denied."

Gorgol's vertical slits of pupils were on him, but he did not acknowledge Hosteen's message. When his rein hand moved, it was in a swift finger wriggle of rejection and denial.

"Logan is with the clan." Hosteen stated that as a fact.

"Logan is of the clan," Gorgol corrected, and so eased Hosteen's worries by a fraction. If the boy was "of the clan," his formal adoption was in force and he was not a prisoner.

"Logan is of the clan," Hosteen agreed. "But he is of the clan of Quade, also. And there is a clan matter he must be concerned with—a task to be done—"

"This is not the season for the herding of frawns or the gathering of horses," Gorgol countered. "The clan goes to the heights on a matter of medicine—"

"We also have our medicine, and no man denies his clan call. I must have speech with Logan on this matter. Would I have ridden into these hills in the Big Dry, I who cannot whistle up the water, were it not a matter of medicine?"

Gorgol was plainly impressed by the sense of that, but when Hosteen would have ridden on, he urged his own mount crosswise to bar the path.

"This is clan talk. Krotag will decide. Until then—you wait."

There was no use in pushing further. Hosteen looked about him. The wait might last an hour—or a day. If he had to stay, he needed protection for the time when the sun would pour down, turning earth and rock into a baking oven. And Gorgol must have read his need, for now the Norbie pulled his mount around.

"Come," he signed. "There is a wait place ahead. But there you must stay."

"There I will stay," Hosteen agreed.

Gorgol's wait place surprised Hosteen. It was a camp site improved by the Norbies, a semipermanent structure of sorts compared to their usual skin-tent villages. Rocks and storm drift, carried along the canyon floor in the Wet Time floods, had been cobbled into an erection large enough to shelter most of a clan, the walls rising above the pit, which gave the coolness of the inner earth to those sweating out the furnace hot hours of the day. Hosteen found more than enough room for his horses, and soon Surra slipped in and Baku swooped down to pick a temporary perch. Hosteen shared out the water and provisions he had renewed at the dump. If he held to the trail marked for him, he would be able to stock up again in two days. But dealing with the clans might throw off his schedule.

He lay on his back on the cool earth and went over their nebulous plans for the hundredth time. Not only would the 'copter lay down dumps ahead, but it should be waiting at their last rendezvous this side of the Peaks to be used in primary exploration for a way through the mountain barrier—providing the Norbies could not or would not guide an off-world party into the Blue.

After a while he must have slept, for he aroused with a start. Surra was pawing at his arm, giving the old signal from their days in the field. She was alerting, not warning, and he expected Gorgol. But the Norbie who dropped down into the shelter was a youngster not yet wearing a hunter's trophy.

"Yuntzil!" Hosteen turned up both thumbs in the warrior's greeting. Gorgol's younger brother was manifestly pleased by this gesture from one wearing warrior's scars, even though of an alien race.

"I see you, one with honorable scars," the boy's slim fingers flashed in the last light of dusk. "I come bearing the signs of Krotag. The Feathered One says: 'There is a time of medicine in the hills, and the fires of friendship burn low. If the brother of our brother rides here, he does so knowing that medicine is a chancy thing and may rend the unbeliever, even as it holds the bow of defense before the believer—"

A warning, but not an outright refusal to allow him to proceed. Hosteen had that much. He stretched his hands into the funnel of light from the doorway so that Yuntzil would have no difficulty in reading the signs he made slowly and with care.

"This one is no unbeliever. To each man his own medicine and the wisdom not to belittle the belief of another. I do not ride under Krotag's medicine, but I have my own." He had taken the precaution that morning before his meeting with Gorgol to put on the heavy turquoise and silver necklace that was part of his inheritance from the past. On their first quest together, when they had faced the Xiks, he had worn that as well as the ketoh bracelet, and he knew that the Norbies now considered both ancient ornaments as talismans of power.

"If the brother of our brother believes, then let him come. He may speak with Krotag."

So they rode through the dusk. But Yuntzil did not keep to the main canyon Hosteen had chosen as the straightest route through the foothills. Perhaps a mile beyond the shelter, he turned abruptly to the left, passed behind an outcrop chimney, and brought the Terran into a narrower way. Surra stayed with Hosteen since the Norbie's mount showed fear of the cat. But Baku was aloft again, and from the eagle Hosteen gained the information that an encampment was not too far ahead.

Silently he thought out his message. To keep the eagle out of sight of any prowling scout, as a set of eyes in reserve, was only a sensible precaution. And he also knew that if and when he gave the order, Surra would melt into the shadows behind them, to be an unseen prowler he would defy any native to locate. She had proved many times in the past that her mutant feline senses were superior to those of any creature, man or animal, that Arzor possessed.

"Now!" As unspoken as his order to Baku, the Terran instructed the dune cat.

The dusk was thick, bringing its coolness after the enervating fire of the day. But ahead was a splotch of light—the camp. Hosteen followed Yuntzil, riding easily. All the horses had been watered before they left the clan shelter, but they quickened their pace, suggesting the necessary liquid was waiting ahead—one of the famous hidden springs, perhaps.

The tall, lean silhouettes of Norbie bodies moved between Hosteen and the fire. He could sight no tent shelters. This might be a scout camp or a hunters' rendezvous, save that Yuntzil had given his invitation in the name of the chief. The young Norbie dismounted, and now he waited, his hand outstretched for Hosteen's reins. If he had noted Surra's disappearance, he did not remark upon it.

Leaving his horses behind him, the Terran walked confidently into the full light of the fire, his sensitive nostrils

47

twitching at the strong, almost unpleasant scent of the burning of bone-dry branches that had been packed from some distance to feed those flames. Falwood, sacred to medicine talks, did not grow in the mountains.

"Hosteen!" A smaller figure separated itself from the tall natives. Like them, he wore the high boots of yoris hide, still attached scales glittering in the greenish light. A wide band of the same hide, this time descaled and softened, made a corselet, covering his body from arm pit to crotch, and over that was the second belt of a warrior from which was suspended the twenty-inch knife of an accepted clansman. Logan had finished off his native dress with the customary yoris-fang collar, which extended from shoulder point to shoulder point and dipped down to belt length across his chest. Above it, his red-brown skin, many shades darker than that of the Norbies, glistened with a sweaty sheen. His head was uncovered, the hair held back from his face by a scarlet band. He was a barbaric figure, somehow more so than the natives about him.

Sighting him free and at ease in the Norbies' camp. Hosteen felt his anxiety and tension crystallize into irritation. He noted the shade of defiance on his half-brother's face, guessed that Logan thought the Terran had come to take him home.

Making no answer to Logan, looking beyond him to the waiting warriors, Hosteen held his hands well into the light of the fire and talked with the deliberate, fully rounded gestures of an envoy.

"There is one who is as the Zamle, whose arrows have drunk blood and their points then been powdered into nothingness many times over, who has hunted the yoris in its den and the evil flyer of the heights, alone, with only the strength of his hands and his medicine. I would speak with that one who stands among you wearing in this life the name of Krotag, leader of warriors, guardian of hunters."

A Norbie moved. The rich beading of his belt glittered more brightly than his scaled leg coverings. His horns, not the ivory-white of the others, were ringed with red.

"There is one named Krotag in this life," his hands acknowledged. "Here he stands. What is wanted of him?"

"Aid." Hosteen's one word answer was, he hoped, enough to intrigue the Norbie's curiosity.

"What manner of aid, man from the river country? You have entered these hills not at our bidding but of your own will. This is a time when those of our blood are to be busied with hidden things. You were warned that this was so—yet still you have come. And now you ask aid. Again I say, what manner of aid?"

"The manner of aid that those of the clans will understand, for this also is a kind they have rendered many times in the past among themselves and to others. Lost in these hills of yours is a stranger—"

Hosteen saw Logan start, but he paid no attention to that reaction.

"Here stand only those of the Zamle feather—and you. We have heard of no stranger lost. In the Big Dry who goes into the heart of the fire?"

"Well asked." Hosteen caught that up. "Who goes into the heart of the fire? Many ask that now—naming clans and tribes!"

Krotag's hands were still. None of the warriors behind him moved. Hosteen wondered if that frankness had been a mistake. But he knew that his motives would be judged by the openness of his speech at this meeting, and totally to ignore the unnatural exodus into the mountains on the part of the clans would be a faulty beginning.

"There are secret things belonging to our people, just as there are secret things that are yours," Krotag signed.

"That is the truth. A man's medicine is his own concern. But it is not of medicine I have come here to speak. It is of an off-world stranger who is lost—"

"Again we say—no such stranger has been spoken of." Krotag's finger exercises were emphatic.

"Not here, not even in the Peaks—"

"Yet you head into this country. Why, since you say that the man you seek is not here?"

"The Peaks are thus." Hosteen made a cup of his left hand; the forefinger of his right ran about the outer ridge of that cup in one swift sweep. "Beyond there is other country—"

It was as if he had brought out of hiding some potent "medicine" of his own, medicine embodied with the power of turning Norbies into pillars of stone as rigid as the canyon walls about them.

"This is the story." The Terran broke into the heart of Widders' tale, refusing to be daunted by the rigid and now unfriendly regard of the natives. With an economy of gesture he told of the reputed landing of the LB, the possible survival of some of those on board. And as he moved his fingers in the complex patterns demanded by that exposition, Hosteen was aware of a change in his audience, a relaxation of tension. They were absorbed in what he had to say, and they believed him. But whether they were willing to give him passage into the Blue on the strength of this was another matter and one, he thought, that would not be settled speedily. He was right about that, for when he had done, Krotag replied.

"This is something to be thought on, brother of our brother. The fire is yours." He stepped aside, his men following his example, leaving a clear passage to the strong-smelling smoke and flames.

Hosteen completed the hospitality ritual, walking on, as he held his breath against gusts of nose-tickling smoke, to take his stand within the circle of heat that was pleasant as a symbol but uncomfortable in fact. When he glanced around, the natives had vanished. Only Logan stood there, watching him levelly with suspicion of hostility.

"You're sharp on the count-off with all this," he commented.

"If you mean this is a piece of fiction designed to get you back, you're off orbit course," Hosteen replied tersely. "It's all true. Widders' men are not now planting supply dumps through the Peaks. He's oath-sure his son is back in the Blue—"

"You aren't goin' to be allowed in there, you know."

Hosteen shook his head. "I don't know, nor do you. They were going to take you with them, weren't they?"

Rather to his surprise Logan shook his head. "I don't know. I only hoped."

"What's going on? Have you any idea?"

"Something that has never happened before and that breaks straight through tribal custom. Hosteen, when you went in with the archaeologist to explore those valley ruins, didn't he have a medicine man for a guide, a Norbie who said that the Old Ones wanted their secrets to be revealed now?"

"Yes. Nothing came of it, though. Those Xik holdouts got the medicine man the same time they wiped out our camp after the big flood."

"But a secret was revealed—we found the Cavern of the Hundred Gardens. Well, the word's out now that the Old Ones are callin' in the clans, plannin' something big. The Norbies have sent out peace poles; every feud has been buried. And the cause is somewhere back in the Blue. But the whole thing is 'medicine.' Let our authorities in, and they will blow it and the tribes wide open. A wrong move now could set every Norbie against us. We'll have to walk small and quiet until we are sure of what we're facin'. I thought Krotag might take me in so I could learn somethin'. I know what those Norbie haters such as Dumaroy could do with a chance to botch up a 'medicine' talk—"

"Which is exactly why 'Asizi is sitting on the blast pin down in the valley now. Didn't think of talking this over with him before you blew, did you?"

Logan flushed. "I know—I know— You think I should have done that. But it doesn't work out—we'd have talked and then maybe argued. We don't think in the same paths. Brad Quake—he's a big man—the kind of man the valley people need. Me—I'm a wild one— I can't want just the holding and building up the herd and being my father's son! Maybe it was the same with Father when he was young. He signed up with Survey, didn't he, and went all over the star lanes? Well, when I was old enough to try somethin' like that, there was the war on— no Survey, and they said I was too young for the Service. So I took to goin' with the Norbies. Sometimes it seems as if they're more my kind than people like Jaffe or Starle.

"Then—well, I guess. I counted too big on that plan of Kelson's for a Ranger force. He promised me the first enlistment in that. It fell through—just like we thought it might. So, maybe I was sore about that. Anyway, I went back to huntin' with the clans—that's how I heard about this.

"And it blew up so suddenly that I knew I didn't dare wait and get in a chew-over about it. I had to ride with the clan then or not at all. The river valley—there's too much talkin' there and not enough doin'! This time I know I was in the right!"

Hosteen shrugged. Argument now was wasted time, and he could understand Logan's frustration. As the younger boy had the wit to see, the inherited strain that had taken Brad Quade into space in his own youth was now working in his son. "I will agree that you did as you thought best. I'm here not about that but for Widders—"

"And to do some nose-pokin' for Kelson—"

"If I make a report to Kelson, that is no more than you were going to do. Think straight, ach'ooni." Deliberately he used the word for brother-friend. "We both know that this situation may hold the seeds of trouble, not only for the settlers but also for the clans. Before, we faced the Xik, and this may be something of the same again. To search for a missing man in the hills is an excuse that the Norbies may accept."

"All right. I'll back you."

"And join me?"

For a moment Logan hesitated. "If they do not turn you back here and now—"

They sat down away from the fire and somewhat ceremoniously shared a drink from Hosteen's canteen, action that would express their present accord to any watching clansmen. As Hosteen rescrewed the cap, Krotag stalked toward them.

"We have thought on this matter of your search." His fingers worked in sharp jerks. "For the time, you ride with us—until we may consult with 'medicine.'"

"As Krotag wishes." Hosteen bowed his head formally and then eyed the chief with a straightness that demanded equality. "As I accede, do you also when the times comes—"

Krotag did not reply. Two youths were throwing sand on the flames. The rest of the men were bringing up their mounts, preparing to ride out.

FIVE

Hosteen smeared the back of his hand across his chin and winced as the cracked and tender skin of his lips reacted to that half-unconscious action. He had given the major portion of his water to the animals, and he had not asked the natives for any of their dwindling supply. Unless within the hour he could strike across the country to the waiting dump, he would be in real trouble. Whether this was a carefully planned move of discouragement on Krotag's part, he did not know, but his suspicions of that were growing. He had no doubts of reaching the cache—Baku's aerial survey would guide him—but soon his mounts would be past rough travel. And trail-tough though he was, Hosteen doubted if a man on foot could make that journey.

Well, there was no use delaying the test any longer. He sent his range horse up along the line of march, past Norbie warriors to Krotag. In the fore he matched pace with the native chief.

"There comes a time for the parting of trails." Hosteen

addressed Krotag with outer assurance. "He who does not whistle water must seek it elsewhere."

"You do not ask it of those who know?"

"In the Big Dry who asks water of friends? It is then more precious than blood. He who sent me to find his son has also sent water—lifting it ahead through the air."

Would Hosteen's policy of the complete truth defeat him now? The air travel of the settlers was unquestioned in the lowlands, tolerated in certain higher districts. But from the first, only one space port had been conceded by the Norbie, who argued that Those-Who-Drum-Thunder in the mountains must not be looked down on from the air. And perhaps a 'copter in these hills would be resented, especially now.

The Terran could read no emotion on the Norbie chieftain's face, though those eyes continued to study him for a long moment. Then fingers moved.

"Where lies this water brought through the sky?"

Following native custom, Hosteen pointed with his chin to a line lying southeast of their present track. Krotag spoke over his shoulder, the shrill twittering bringing out of line and cantering ahead two warriors, followed by Logan.

"No one may deny water when it can be found." Krotag repeated the first law of his people. "But this is country in which the wild ones roam, and you have many horses. So it is wise that you do not ride alone. These shall be added bows." With a thumb jerk he indicated the measure of security in Krotag's choice. Both were familiar natives.

Gorgol and his own son Kavok—Hosteen felt a small measure of security in Krotag's choice. Both were familiar

56

with settler ways, had ridden for Quade. Once he had thought that he was on a basis of friendship with Gorgol, though the happenings of the past days had made the Terran more wary of claiming any sure standing with the young warrior.

Logan crowded his mount forward. "I would ride, too."

Again Krotag appeared to consider the point before he gave assent. Then the native line plodded on in the evening dusk just as they had ridden through the two nights since Hosteen had joined them, while he drew aside his horses, the extra mounts and the pack mares. Surra, responding to his suggestion, was already ranging along the side gully they must use to cut back to the wider canyon up which Quade and he had planned his entrance into the Blue.

The overland trail was rough, and at night they had to take it slowly. Logan rode beside Hosteen.

"How far are we from this dump?"

"I don't know—maybe a day. Depends upon the angle of the split when I joined the clansmen."

"We'll have to hole up in the day—"

That was what had been plaguing Hosteen as the hours crawled by. He searched all the latter part of the night for some feature of the countryside that could be adapted for a sun shelter, and he was not alone in that search, for Gorgol and Kavok rode with the width of the gorge between them, as if looking for some landmark.

There was a twittering call from Kavok, which, though they could not understand its import, brought the settlers to him. The young Norbie had dismounted and was down on one knee, running his hand along what looked to Hosteen to be undisturbed surface soil. Then he walked

57

ahead, leading his horse, as if he followed some very faint trail.

They came away from the main cut they had taken into a side ravine, which slanted sharply upward. Kavok went down on his knees once more and dug into the side of the ravine with his long hunting knife, an occupation in which Gorgol speedily joined him, leaving Hosteen and Logan completely mystified.

Surra flowed down the side of the cut. She stopped short a yard or so away from the hole the two Norbies had already excavated, and nose wrinkled, she growled deep in her throat. Gorgol glanced over his shoulder, sighted the cat, and touched Kavok, nodding from Surra to the excavation. Hosteen caught the sudden surge of hunting interest from the feline mind. Beyond the flying knives, the busy hands of the natives, there was something alive, and that quarry was attracting all Surra's feral love of the chase and the kill.

The earth under the scraping hands of the Norbies suddenly caved in, and both of them jerked back as a hole appeared, growing wider as if they had laid bare an underground chasm. Their knives were still at ready, but not to dig, rather to defend themselves against attack. Hosteen, warned by their attitude, drew his stunner. Gorgol flung out a hand in a gesture of waiting.

Surra, her belly fur brushing loose earth, the tip of her tail twitching with anticipation, crept forward with feline caution, her broad paws placed and then lifted in succession with the precision of the stalking huntress.

The Norbies gave her room, and Hosteen lost mind touch. Now the big cat was all hunting machine, not to be turned from the chase. She would answer to no order or suggestion while in this state. Her furred head, fox-sharp ears pricked, hung out over the opening. Then, as if she were melting into the loose sand and earth, she was gone, down into the unseen pit the Norbies had opened.

Gorgol squatted back on his haunches, and Hosteen caught at his shoulder in a tight and demanding grip.

"What lies below?" the Terran demanded.

"Djimbut pit!" Logan replied before Gorgol could raise a hand to answer.

"Djimbut?" Hosteen repeated, unable to connect the word with anything he knew. Then he remembered a pelt of close-curled black fur, as beautiful in its way as the frawn hides, which served as a wall hanging back in Quade's Basin holding. But that had been the skin of a big beast—one close to Surra in size. Was the Terran cat about to attack such an animal in its own den?

He elbowed Gorgol aside and recklessly launched himself feet first into the hole, one hand holding the stunner close to his chest, the other fumbling for his atom torch as he slid into darkness.

Hosteen landed with a jar on a heap of sand and earth. He crouched there, listening for any sound, becoming more and more conscious of the coolness of this place. He even shivered slightly as he pushed the button of the torch and discovered that he was in the center of a hollowed area of some size.

As the Terran slued about on the sand pile, the narrow beam of the torch swept across a tunnel mouth large enough to give Surran passage or to accommodate a man on his hands and knees. Hosteen scrambled for that, again to crouch in its entrance listening.

Sounds came clearly enough—growl, rounding out into

a spitting, yowling challenge that was the dune cat's. Then, in answer, a queer kind of hum ending in a series of coughing grunts, broken by what could only be sounds of battle, enjoined and fiercely fought. Somewhere beyond, that tunnel must widen into a passage or chamber big enough to provide a field for a desperate struggle. Hosteen was head and shoulders into the passage when the coughing grunts deepened into a weird moaning, which was clipped off short. And into his mind came the vivid impression of Surra's triumph, just as his ears caught a singsong rise and fall, which she uttered to proclaim her victory aloud.

Three yards, a little more, and he was in another chamber. Here the smell of blood combined with a thick, musky scent. His light beam caught Surra kneading with her forepaws a rent and blood-sticky heap of fur, her eyes yellow balls of nonhuman joy when the light caught them. She sat upright as Hosteen knelt beside her, tonguing herself where a long red scratch ran across her shoulder. But her battle hurts were few and ones she herself would tend.

The Terran flashed his light about to discover a series of openings in the walls, and his nostrils took in not only the hot blood scent and the odor of the dead animal but also other smells issuing from some of those holes. The place was large—whether the result of the djimbut's burrowing or because the animal had located and used some natural fault in the earth, he was not sure. But he was able to get to his feet and stand with the roof of the chamber still well above his head. And the space, apart from the other openings, was at least ten by twenty feet, he estimated.

Surra gave a last lick to her wound scratch and then

hunkered down to sniff along the battered body on the floor, growling and favoring the corpse with a last vindictive slap of forepaw. Hosteen centered the torch on the black bundle. The dead creature was as large as Surra, perhaps a fraction bigger, the chunky body equipped with four legs, which were short and clawed, the talons on the forelimbs being great sickle-shaped armaments he would not have wanted to face. But the head was the alien feature as far as the Terran was concerned. The skull was rounded without visible ears. In fact, as he leaned forward to inspect it more closely, Hosteen had difficulty in identifying eyes—until he glimpsed a round white bulb half concealed by thick curls of fur. The lower part of that head—the mouth and jaws—was broad and flat, tapering into a thin wedge at the outmost point, as if the creature had been fitted by nature with a tooth-rimmed chisel for a mouth.

"Djimbut all right." Logan made a hands and knees progress into the big chamber. "Surra did for him—good girl."

Those yellow eyes half closed as the dune cat looked at Logan. Then a rumble of a purr answered his frank praise.

"We're in luck," Logan continued. "Got us about the best waitout anyone could find in these hills—"

And that had been the reason for the action Hosteen discovered. The lair of the djimbut was not just the tunnel and its two connected chambers. It was also a series of storerooms opening off the big room, an underground dwelling so constructed as to be heat-proof even when they had to wreck most of the protected opening to get the horses under cover.

The damp chill faded, but the men and the Norbies quartered in the storerooms and the horses in the main chamber had a hideout from the sun that was the best protection Hosteen had found since he left the outer valley. And the seeds and roots stored up were sorted over by the natives, a selection given to and relished by their mounts and the rest taken over by their riders.

Hosteen chewed at a yellow-green pod. The flint surface splintered, giving him a mouthful of pulp, which had refreshing moisture. Gleams of sun reached them through the broken walls, but they were well out of its full heat, and they dozed off for the day.

The Terran did not know just what brought him awake with the old, instant awareness of his Service days. His head, resting on earth, might have picked up the vibration of a distant tread. He levered himself up in the cubby he shared with Logan, hearing the restless movements of the horses. A mind cast for Surra told him that the cat was either not in range or deliberately refusing to answer. But the patches of sky he could see were those of early evening. And somewhere beyond, there were riders approaching.

Hosteen's hand went out to cover Logan's mouth as the younger settler slept on his back, bringing him to silent wakefulness. In answer to the question in the other's eyes, the Terran motioned to the outer chamber.

Together they crawled out among the horses to discover Gorgol before them, his hand gripping the nose of his own mount to discourage any welcoming nicker. That told Hosteen what he wanted to know. With his free hand he signed, "Enemy?" and was answered by a vigorous assent from the Shosonna.

They were certainly not in any good position to meet an attack. To get the horses up out of the burrow again was a difficult task at best, and to be jumped while so employed— Hosteen made a mind cast for Surra. He was sure the cat had already left the djimbut burrow. Baku must have flown on to the cache and be waiting there for them. She had not returned the evening before, and her wings made her free from the toilsome march the rest must take. But with Surra one part of the team was still in reach.

"Who—?" He turned to Gorgol for enlightenment.

"Wild ones."

"The peace poles are up," Logan's hands protested.

Gorgol tossed his head in the equivalent of a human shrug.

"These may be far-back ones—they want horses."

The Shosonna and other lowland tribes had their own methods of recruiting their studs. Their young men hiring out as herd riders, their yoris hunters, could trade for the horses they wanted to build up clan herds. For the wild Norbies of the high country, envious of their fellows but fearful of venturing down to contact the settlers, there was another way of acquiring the wonder animals to which the Arzoran native-born had taken with the same ease and fierce joy that Hosteen's own Amerindian ancestors had welcomed the species when the Europeans introduced them to the western continental plains. The wild ones were horse thieves of constantly increasing skill.

And to such thieves, the trail of this party must have been a heady inducement. Any experienced tracker crossing their traces would know that four riders had a total of nine horses with them, counting the pack horses

63

and extra mounts—a windfall not even the raising of a peace pole could save. And here the enemy could simply wait them out with lack of water as the lever to pry them from their refuge.

Which left only Surra. Hosteen said as much, and Gorgol twittered to Kavok before he signed:

"The furred one is not here. Kavok saw her go when the sun was still a sky bead. Perhaps she is beyond your call—"

Hosteen leaned against the now crumbling wall of the burrow, closed his eyes, and threw all his strength and energy into one long call, noiseless, quick, and, he hoped, far reaching enough to touch minds with the cat.

With the snap of one pressing an activating button on a com and receiving an answer, he made the break-through. There were the few moments of seeming to see the world slightly askew and weirdly different—which told him that they had made contact. Then he gave his instructions and had agreement from Surra. Distance meant little to her, and her form of reckoning was not that of a man. He could not tell how far she now was from the wrecked burrow nor how long it would take her to track down the enemy, waiting out there, and deliver the counterstroke that could mean the difference between life and death for those underground. But before she went into action, she would report.

"Surra is movin' in?" Logan asked in a half whisper.

Hosteen nodded. The strain of making that contact was still on him. Gorgol's head was up, his finely cut nostrils expanded.

"They are all about us," he reported.

"How many?" Hosteen demanded.

The smooth head, its ivory horns seeming to gleam in the gathering twilight, swung in a slow side-to-side motion before the Norbie answered:

"Four—five—" He flicked one finger after another as he located the raiders with his own kind of built-in radar. "Six—"

That finger count reached ten before it stopped. Cramped as they were in this earth bottle, those odds seemed impossible. Kavok had no arm room to use his bow. And while Logan and Hosteen had stunners and Gorgol another that had been Hosteen's gift on their first war path months earlier, the weapon of the settlers was a defensive device for which one had to see a good target.

Surra was ready!

Hosteen signed a warning. Kavok had dropped his useless bow, drawn his knife. Leaving the horses, they pushed to the foot of the improvised ramp down which they had brought those animals in the early morning.

"Now!" Hosteen's lips writhed in an exaggerated movement that he knew Gorgol would recognize. At the same time his order flashed to the waiting cat.

Surra's shrill, ear-splitting scream tore the air. In answer came the terrified neighing of horses, not only from behind but also from the opening ahead. They heard the drum of racing hoofs and the high twittering of Norbie cries.

Hosteen broke for the ramp. Outside, he rolled behind a rock, then pulled himself up to survey the ravine. Surra yowled again, and he saw a figure with blue-dyed horns stand recklessly out in the open fitting arrow to bow cord. The Terran thumbed his stunner button and beamed the narrow ray for the skull wearing those blue horns. The

Norbie wilted to the ground in a lank fold-up of long, thin arms and legs.

Another broke from cover, thrusting into the open, his head turned on his shoulders, his whole body expressing his terror as Surra's head and forequarters rose into view. The cat ducked back into cover as Hosteen fired again. Surra was doing her part—driving the wild tribesmen into the waiting fire like the expert she was in this form of warfare.

SIX

Gorgol stooped above one of the still Norbies and lifted the head from the gravel by a painted horn.

"Nitra," he identified.

Kavok thrust a booted toe under another of the attackers and rolled him over.

"They still live—" he commented, fingering his knife as he surveyed the limp body, his thoughts as plain as if he had shouted them aloud in Galactic basic.

Warrior trophies were warrior trophies. On the other hand, these unconscious enemies, now flat on sand and gravel or looped over the rocks where they had been stun-rayed as they tried to evade Surra, were by custom the property of those who had brought them down. Hosteen, Logan, and Gorgol had the sole right to collect horn tips to display at a Shosonna triumph drumming.

"Let them remain so," Hosteen signed to both Norbies. "The peace poles are up. If the Nitra break the laws of Those-Who-Drum-Thunder, do the Shosonna also work evil?"

Kavok thrust his knife back into its sheath. "What then do we? Leave these to recover from your medicine fire so that they may trail us to try again?"

"The cool of night will be gone and the sun rising before they wake from their sleep," the Terran answered. "And we take their horses. They must make day refuge in the burrow or die. I do not think they will try to follow us."

"That is true," Gorgol agreed. "And also it is right that we do not break the peace. Let us be on our way that we may find your water place before *we* greet the sun."

The mounts of the Nitra had been prevented from bolting by Surra's presence down canyon. Now, sweating and rolling their eyes fearfully, they were caught and fastened to the horses of Hosteen's pack train. And the party was well on its way across country, leaving its late opponents slumbering by the ruins of the djimbut burrow, before the night had completely closed in.

In the false dawn they came upon Widders' dump, where a section of the far tip of Finger Canyon widened out. The Norbies whistled in surprise, for they fronted a bubble tent of plastaglau, its blue-gray surface opaque and heat-resistant. From a rock beyond, Baku took off to fly to Hosteen. There was no other sign of life there.

Logan glowered at the off-world mushroom squatting arrogantly on Arzoran earth.

"So—what does this civ think we are? Pampered pets from the inner worlds?"

The Terran shrugged. "What he thinks does not matter—it may be that he considers this to be necessary shelter. What he brings is more important—we need those supplies."

But he, too, was startled by that tent, unwanted and unreal in its present setting. It gave the appearance of more than just a dump, though their plans had not called for any base here.

"You say we ride for water—this is an off-world live place!" Kavok's protest came on snapping fingers. Hosteen disliked the hostility in that outburst. Widders had made just the stupid mistake that settlers on Arzor tried to avoid. Some off-world equipment and weapons the Norbies accepted as a matter of course. But a strange dwelling set down in the heart of their own territory without any agreement beforehand—that was an aggravation that, in the present precariously balanced state of affairs, might well send them all packing out of the Peaks—at the very best. Why Kelson had allowed Widders to commit this might-be-fatal mistake Hosteen could not understand.

He came up to the plasta-glau hemisphere and smacked his hand with more than necessary force against the close lock, taking out some of his irritation in that blow. There was a shimmer of fading forcefield, and he could see the small cubby of the heat lock open before him.

This thing imported from off-world must have cost a small fortune. To set up camp here did not make sense, and things that did not make sense were suspicious. Hosteen's foot pressure on the bal-floor of the lock activated the forcefield, sealing him in before a second barrier went down, making him free of the interior.

Perhaps this was only a utility bubble, intended for what an inner-planet man would consider the most rustic living, Hosteen thought, for there was only one big room. The supplies he sought were piled in boxes and containers in its center. But around the slope-walled perimeter he saw fold beds—four of them!—a cook unit, a drink unit, and even a portable refresher! No, this could not have been intended as a one-day camp!

He persuaded the Norbies to enter, brought in the horses, and set up a line of supply boxes to mark off a temporary stable, since that was one need the designer of the bubble had apparently not foreseen. The quarters for settlers and natives were correspondingly cramped, but Hosteen knew they could weather the day now with more comfort than they had known even in the depths of the burrow.

Gorgol and Kavok examined their new housing with suspicion, gradually overcome by interest. They were already familiar with the conveniences of cook and drink units, and having seen Hosteen and Logan make use of the refresher, they tried it in turn.

"This is a fine thing," Kavok signed. "Why not for Norbie, too?" He looked inquiringly at the settlers, and Hosteen guessed the young native was trying to reckon in his mind the amount of trade goods it might take to purchase such a wonder for the clan.

"This be a fine thing—but see—" Hosteen opened the control box of the cook unit, displaying an intricate pattern of wiring. "Do this break, one man maybe in Galwadi, he could fix—maybe he could not. Some pieces might have to come from beyond the stars. Then what good is this?"

Kavok digested that and agreed. "No good. Many yoris skins, many frawn skins to be paid for this?"

"That is so. Quade, our blood-father" he made the sign for clan chief—"he is a man of many horses, many fine things from beyond the stars. That is so?"

"That is so," the Shosonna agreed.

"Yet, Quade, our blood-father, he could drive all his horses and half his frawn herd in the Peaks to the Port, and there he would have to give them all up for a place such as this, a place that, when it broke, no man could have mended without giving many more horses, many frawn hides—"

"Then this is not a good thing!" Kavok's reaction was quick and emphatic. "Why is this here now?"

"The off-world one who seeks his son, he is not used to the Big Dry, and he thinks that one cannot live—as perhaps he could not—without such a thing."

"He is truly an off-world child of little knowledge," was Kavok's comment.

Baku sidled along the edge of a box she had selected for a perch. Now she mantled, her wings a quarter spread, and gave a throaty call. Surra was already at the door.

"Company." Hosteen drew his stunner. But somehow he did not believe they were about to face another native raiding party. Baku's warning was of an air approach, and he expected a 'copter.

What he did not foresee as he strode out to the patch of ground already bearing the marks of several landings and take-offs, was the size of the flyer making an elevator descent there. The 'copters, used sparingly by the settlers because of the prohibitive cost of replacement parts and repairs, were able, at best, to hold three or four men crowded together, with a limited space for emergency supplies or very valuable cargo. The machine now agleam in the early-morning light was a sleek, expensive type such as Hosteen had never seen on any frontier world. And his estimation of Widders' wealth and influence went up again. To transport such a craft to Arzor must have cost a small fortune. No wonder that with such a carrier the civ had been able to send in a bubble tent and all the other trappings of a real safari.

Nor was the Terran too amazed to see Widders himself descend the folding ladder from the flyer's cockpit. He had at least changed his off-world clothing for more durable coveralls such as a pilot wore. And he had belted about his slight paunch an armory of gadgets such as Hosteen had not seen since he mustered out of the Service.

"So you finally got here!" Widders greeted him sourly. Glancing around, he added in a petulant spurt of words, "Where're all those horses you were sure we needed so badly?"

"In there." Hosteen nodded toward the tent and was amazed at the answering flood of dusky color on the other's craggy face.

"You—put—animals—in—my—tent!"

"I don't lose horses, not when our lives depend on them," the Terran retorted. "Nor would I sentence any living thing to a day in the sun during the Big Dry! Your pilot had better taxi over under that overhang if he wants to save this 'copter. At this hour you can not hope to get back to the nearest plains shelter—"

"I have no intention of returning to the plains region," Widders replied, and he meant that. Short of picking him up bodily, Hosteen realized, and putting him forcibly into the 'copter, there was no way of shipping him out—for now.

However, one day in the crowded and now rather stale-smelling interior of the tent might well induce the civ to reconsider his decision. There was no use wasting energy fighting a wordy battle now when time and nature might convince him. Hosteen relayed his warning to the pilot and left the civ to enter the tent by himself.

When he came in with the pilot, an ex-Survey man who held tightly to a position of neutrality, Hosteen walked into tension, though there were as yet no outwardly hostile gestures or words. Widders swung around to face the Terran, the dusky hue of his face changed to a livid fury.

"What is the meaning of this—this madhouse?"

"This is the Big Dry, and during the day you get under cover or you cook. I mean that literally." Hosteen did not raise his voice, but his words were delivered with force. "You can really bake to death out among those rocks. You wanted native guides—this is Kavok, son to Krotag, chief of the Zamle clan of the Shosonna, and Gorgol, a warrior of the same clan, also my brother, Logan Quade. I don't know any better help we can get for Peak exploration."

He watched the struggle mirrored on Widders' face. The man's natural arrogance had been affronted, but his necessary dependence on Hosteen prevailed. He loathed the situation, but for the moment there was nothing he could do to remedy it. His acceptance came, however, with poor grace.

The Norbies and the settlers luxuriated in the conditioned temperature of the bubble, but Hosteen wondered privately just how much overloading the conditioner could take. Widders probably had the best. But no one from off-world could possibly realize the demands of the Big Dry unless they experienced them firsthand.

"Storm!" He roused at that peremptory hail from the bunk Widders had chosen some hours earlier.

Stretching, Hosteen sat up and reached for his boots. He, Logan, and the pilot had taken the other bunks. The Norbies had chosen to use their rolled sleep mats on the floor.

"What is it?" he asked now, without too much interest in what he expected would be Widders' complaints, his mind more occupied with what Krotag might feel if he came upon this camp without explanation. They were only here on sufferance, and the Shosonna could well force them back into the lowlands.

"I want to know what plans you have made for getting us back into the Blue."

Hosteen stood up. Both Gorgol and Kavok were awake, their attention switching from Widders to the Terran and back again. Though the Norbies could not understand the words of the off-world men, they could, as Hosteen had learned in the past, often make surprisingly accurate guesses as to the subject of conversation.

"Plans? Gentle Homo, on an expedition such as this, you cannot make definite plans ahead. A situation may change quickly. So far, we are here—but even to remain here is in question." He went on to outline what they might fear from Krotag, making plain that the camp itself could arouse the ire of the natives. "So—it must be as we originally decided, Gentle Homo—you will return to the lowlands."

"No." Flat, nonequivocal. And again Hosteen understood that he might, with some expenditure of force, remove the civ from this camp, but he could not give the order to raise the 'copter and fly Widders back to the river lands. The pilot would not obey him. On the other hand, the Terran's best answer, to wash his hands of the matter completely and go back himself, was impossible, too. He could not leave Widders on his own here to cross the natives and perhaps provide the very reason for the trouble Quade and Kelson were laboring to avoid, that Logan had risked his life to stop. Widders sensed Hosteen's position, for he rapped out:

"Now—where do we go from this point, Storm?"

He unhooked a small box, one of the many items looped to that fantastic belt of his, and held it before him, thumbing a lever on its side.

On the wall of the bubble tent appeared a map of this region of the Peaks, containing all the settlers knew of the country. Hosteen caught a twittering exclamation from Kavok, saw Gorgol eye the lines. The latter had some map lore gathered as a rider.

Time—Hosteen decided—was the factor now. Even if Krotag ordered them out, the chief had yet to reach them to do so. The Terran addressed the pilot.

"How well is the 'copter shielded? Can you take it up before sundown?"

"Why?" demanded Widders. "We have a direct find on board."

A direct find! Now how had Widders managed to have such an installation released to him? So far as Hosteen knew, those were service issue only. But that machine, which would center on any object within a certain radius, did cut down the element of time loss in search to a high degree.

"Can you take off before sundown?" Hosteen persisted. It was not the possible loss of time in sweeping an unfamiliar territory in search of the LB wreck that worried him now—but how long they might have before Krotag or other Norbies sighted this camp.

"We're shielded to the twelfth degree." That admission came with visible reluctance from the pilot. Hosteen did not blame him. Flying in a twelve-degree shield was close to the edge of acute discomfort. But that was his problem, and he could refuse if he wanted to—let Widders and his hired fly-boy fight it out between them.

"What's all this about shielding?" Widders broke in.

Hosteen explained. If the 'copter was shielded so that the pilot dared to take off before dusk, then they could make one flight over the edge of the Blue at once, before the coming of any Norbies. Widders grabbed at the chance.

"We *can* lift now?" He rounded on Forgee, the pilot.

"*We?*" repeated Hosteen. "Do you propose to go also, Gentle Homo?"

"I do." Again that adamant refusal to consider anything else expressed in every line of his face and body. Widders set the map broadcaster down on a supply box and advanced, to thrust a forefinger violently into the picture so that the shadow of his hand blotted out a fourth of the territory. "Right here—your officials have pinpointed the LB broadcast as best they could."

Gorgol scrambled to his feet, his twittering squeaked high. Momentarily, the Norbie had foresaken finger speech to register angry protest in his native tongue. Then, as if he recollected the limitations of the off-worlders, he flexed his fingers before him and began a series of gestures so swift and intricate that Hosteen had difficulty in reading them.

76

"This off-world man wishes to go *there?* But that is not for strangers—it is medicine—the medicine of those who eat THE MEAT— This cannot be done!"

"What does he say?" Widders demanded.

"That that is cannibal territory and dangerous—" But Hosteen was certain Gorgol feared more than cannibals.

"We knew all that before we came." Widders was contemptuous. "Does he think his cannibals can bring a 'copter down by bows and arrows?"

Forgee stirred. "Look here, Gentle Homo, this Blue is tricky. Air currents in there have never been charted. And what we do know about them is enough to make a man think twice about trying to get very far in."

"We have every safety device built into that flyer that human ingenuity can or has devised," Widders flared, "including quite a few that never reached this back-water world before. Come—let's take off and see for ourselves what this Blue is like."

Kavok half crouched by the doorway. His knife was out and ready in his hand, his enmity so openly displayed that Hosteen was startled.

"What—?" The Terran's hand sign was addressed to Gorgol, and the Norbie replied, less swiftly, with the attitude of one pushed into a corner.

"Medicine—big medicine. The off-worlder cannot go there. If he tries, he will die."

"That answers it." For the first time Logan entered the conversation. "Gorgol says that is medicine country—you can't fly over it now."

Widders' contempt was plain as he raked Logan from head to foot in one long stare of measurement and dismissal, assessing the other's Norbie dress and rating him low because of wearing it. Under that stare Logan flushed angrily, but when he moved, it was to stand beside Kavok by the door, his hand hovering over the butt of his stunner.

"That is true." Hosteen spoke carefully, his position now, he thought, that of a very thin and breakable wall between two male yoris at mating season. "There is no arguing with 'medicine.' If the Norbies have declared that country out of bounds for such a reason, we *are* stopped."

He had never underrated Widders' determination and self-confidence, he had only underrated the man's recourse to action. Widders did not go for his stunner, a move that would have alerted them. Instead he snapped a small pellet to the floor of the tent at a point midway between Hosteen and Gorgol and the two now guarding the door. A flash of light answered—then nothing, nothing at all.

SEVEN

"—calling District Station Peaks—come in—D.S. Peaks—come in!"

There was a frantic note in that repetition that reached Hosteen through the fog in his head. He was also aware of moisture on his cheek and the rasp of a rough tongue. He opened his eyes to discover Surra crouched over him, striving to bring him back to consciousness by her own method.

Gorgol and Kavok sat on the floor, their elbows propped on their bent knees, each with his head between his hands. Beyond them, Logan was up on a swing seat pulled out from the table, one hand to his head, the other holding the call mike of a com to his lips as he got out, between gasping breaths not far removed from moans, his air appeal—

"D.S. Peaks—come in! Come in!"

As Hosteen squirmed up to a sitting position, a red-hot lance of pain cut through his head just behind his eyeballs. And every movement, no matter how cautious, brought on another throb of that agony. He had been stun-rayed once, but this was worse than the after effects of a blasting from that most common of stellar weapons. To get to his feet was an action beyond his powers of endurance, but he managed to slide across to the table edge, to look up at Logan.

"What—are—you—doing?" The shaping of words brought on further pain, and he wondered at Logan's persistence in trying to use the com.

His half-brother glanced down, eyes wide and pain-filled in a face that was a mirror for the punishment he was taking.

"Widders took off—in 'copter—trouble—" Logan's hand dropped from his head and gripped the edge of the table until his knuckles stood out as pale knobs.

Hosteen remembered and began to think again with some measure of clarity. Widders had knocked them all out with an off-world gadget, then had taken off in the 'copter, flying straight for the forbidden territory. The Norbies could and probably would be affronted enough by the invasion of their medicine country to retaliate. And settlers such as Dumaroy would return any attack from the natives without trying to negotiate. A fire might have been kindled here and now that would sear this whole world as fatally as Terra had been scorched by the Xik blast.

The Terran hitched away from the table, biting his lip against the torture inside his skull, managing to reach Gorgol. The Norbie's eyelids were tightly closed; there was a thin beading of moisture along the hairless arch of his forehead. It was plain he was feeling all that Hosteen did, if not more, since one could not assess the reaction of alien physiology to an off-world weapon.

But there was no time to waste in useless sympathy. Hosteen touched the native's forearm with all the gentleness he could muster. There was a whistle of sound from Gorgol. His eyes came open and moved in their sockets to focus on the Terran as if he dared not try to turn his head.

Somehow Hosteen balanced himself in that hunched position so that he could free his hands for talking.

"The off-worlder has gone. We must—"

He was not allowed to finish. Gorgol's head thumped back against the wall of the tent. He gave a small, stifled trill, and then his fingers moved in answer:

"He has done evil—much evil—and we have allowed it. There will be a judging—"

"I have done evil." Hosteen signed. "For it is I who listened to his story and brought him here—though I did not know he would come. You carry no blame in this matter—none of us knew that he would attack us to get his desire—"

"He flies the sky thing into the medicine country. Those-Who-Drum-Thunder, loose the lightning arrows, will be swelling in their wrath. This is not good—evil! Evil!" To finger signs Gorgol added a thin wailing of his own untranslatable vocal sounds.

Kavok's eyes opened. He spat with much the same hissing hate as Surra mustered upon proper occasion. But before Gorgol could continue, they were interrupted by words—spoken in good Galactic basic—issuing from the mike Logan still held.

"TRI calling base camp—" There was a smug note in

that voice that aroused Hosteen's temper to the point of seething. "TRI calling base camp—"

He lurched across the space between wall and table, fighting off the sickness the pain of that effort cost him. Then he wrenched the mike away from Logan and leaned weakly against the table edge as he called:

"Widders!"

"So—you've come around!" The voice out of the air held a trace of amusement that did nothing to dampen the Terran's temper.

Hosteen fought for control, achieved enough to demand:

"Are you already into the Blue, Widders?"

"On our way right up to that check point. How's your headache, Storm? Told you I was doing this myself—I know *my* business—"

"Widders—listen, man—turn back—turn back right now!" The Terran knew even as he made that plea he was urging uselessly. But in that 'copter was the pilot, and surely Forgee had been long enough on Arzor, had been well enough trained by Survey, to realize the danger of what they were doing. "Forgee—don't be a fool! Get back in a hurry. You're beraking 'medicine'—not just of one clan, but of all the tribes! Turn back before they spot you. You can be planet-banned for a stunt like this—"

"My, Storm, that headache must be a bad one," Widders began lightly. Then the steel ripped out of the sheath as he added: "These natives won't even see us—I have a shield force up—and we are going in to the check point. Nobody—nobody, Storm—is telling me what I may or may not do when my son's life may be at stake. We'll keep you informed. TRI signing off—"

There was the click of a broken connection. Hosteen put down the mike. He looked at Logan, and the younger man's face was drawn, sickly pallid under its weathering.

"He's going right ahead—"

Gorgol was on his feet, standing unsteadily with one hand braced against the wall of the tent. With the other he signed:

"Krotag—we ride for Krotag—"

"No!" Hosteen answered and saw the stiffness in Gorgol's expression. The Terran indicated the mike. "We call the Peace Officer. He will bring in the law—"

"Off-world law!" Gorgol's whole body expressed his contempt.

Logan pushed away from the table and stood, weaving, yet free of support, using both hands. His Norbie dress did not look strange as he gestured, and the smooth flow of his signs was akin to the ceremonial speech of a chief meeting.

"Last wet season there was Hadzap, who came down into the herds of Quade, not asking for hunter's rights—which those of Quade's clan would have freely granted as is the custom. But he came in secret, without speech, and slew, taking only hides. And these he carried to the Port and would have sold to off-world men, asking for those things that he believed would make him greater in the clan. Was this not a shame upon all those of the Zamle totem? Yet did Quade's clansmen come to take Hadzap for judging under off-world laws? No—not so. Quade sent me to Krotag to ask for speech between one clan chief and another as is rightful custom. And Krotag replied— let it be so—you, Kavok, riding with me to report to

Quade as was right and proper, for we are both sons to chiefs.

"Then Quade came and Krotag, and they sat down together. Quade telling of what had been done. But when he had finished, he rode out to your camp leaving Hadzap to the justice of Krotag, nor did he afterwards inquire what punishment had been set—for this is as it should be when chief deals with chief. Is this not so?"

"That is so," assented both Norbies.

"You may say now that this evil committed by an offworlder is greater than the evil wrought by Hadzap. In that you are right. But do not think that we do not also consider it an evil. Did not this person of no totem strike us down also, for he knew that we would have prevented him by force from what he would do. And the Peace Officer will deal with him after our laws, even as Hadzap was dealt with by yours, for this is a grievous act and one that will harm both settlers and Norbies."

"This is truth," Gorgol agreed. "Yet Krotag must be told—for he gave you the right to ride here, and he, also, will be answerable to others for this evil act."

"That is so," Hosteen agreed. "Let one of you ride for Krotag, and we shall remain here, trying to call our Peace Officer through the air talker—"

"And you swear it on the blood that you will wait here?" Gorgol looked from Hosteen to Logan. "Yes, it is so, for you are not of those who give their word and then make nothing of it for reasons of their own. I ride—let Kavok stay—since other than Zamle men may come and he can talk under the truce pole should that be needful."

They took alternate shifts at the com after Gorgol departed, trying to reach the Peaks office with their calls—

but silence was their only answer. Nor did Hosteen's periodic demands upon the 'copter bring any reply from Widders or Forgee. The Terran tried to deduce how far into the Blue the flyer could go before the two would have to return to escape the day heat—without much success.

"They could even set down somewhere in there and take cover," Logan pointed out.

"Once a fool, always a fool—that's what you think of the civ? That's cannibal territory—he's been warned—"

"Widders is the type who wouldn't expect any danger from natives," Logan retorted. "And he's armed with about every possible defensive gadget he could find. I wouldn't put it past him to have smuggled a blaster in on that 'copter! He'd believe he could stand off any Norbie attack."

And Logan was entirely right. Widders would think himself invulnerable as a modern, civilized man coping with natives armed only with primitive weapons. But, as all civs from off-world, he would thereby seriously underestimate the Norbies if he relied on mechanics to defeat those who had mastered nature in the Arzoran outback.

"Sleeee—" The hissing whistle cut through the open door of the bubble tent and startled both men.

Hosteen went out. There had been no alert from Baku or Surra, which meant the newcomers must be known to both member of the team. But he was angry at himself for not having briefed both cat and bird to give warning of any arrival.

It was not until the riders filed out of shadows into the open floor of the canyon that Hosteen recognized Krotag heading a party of warriors. The Terran waited in the path of light from the doorway, not advancing to meet the chief when he dismounted. He must take his cue from Krotag. This was no time for excuses or explanations. The native leader must have had the story from Gorgol—and he must already have been on his way here or he would not have arrived so soon after the messenger left. What action he would take was his decision, and according to custom Hosteen must wait for the Norbie's verdict.

The Terran stepped back as Krotag came up, allowing the chief to enter the tent, and then he gave way for a second tall figure.

Unlike the warriors, this native wore no arms belt or protective shield collar of yoris fangs. Instead, his bony frame was covered with a striking tunic fashioned of black-and-white feathers woven skillfully into a net foundation of frawn yarn. His horns were stained dead black, and each of his deep-set eyes were encircled by an inch-wide ring of black paint, which gave his face a skull-like aspect, daunting to the beholder. In addition to his feather tunic, he wore a short knee-length cloak, also a feathered net, but this of a brilliant yellow-green. And around his neck, on white cords, was slung a small black drum.

"I see you who wears the name of Krotag." Hosteen signed formal salutation.

"I see you—stranger—"

Not a good beginning, but one he had to accept. Hosteen looked at the Drummer.

"I see also the one who can summon the bright sky arrows," he continued. "And this one also wears a name?"

Silence, so complete that they could hear from outside the stir of a horse. Then the Drummer's hands came out before him, palms up, while those black-ringed eyes caught and held Hosteen's in a compelling stare.

Hardly aware of his action, the Terran raised his own hands, moved them out until palm met palm, and so they stood linked by the touch of flesh against flesh, Hosteen and the Norbie medicine man. Once before in his life the Amerindian had felt a power, not human and far beyond the control of any man, fill and move him. Then he had been swept up and used by that power to bring prisoners out of a Nitra camp. But at that time he had deliberately evoked the "medicine" of his own people. And now—

Words came out of him, words the Drummer could not understand—or could he?

> *"I have a song—and an offering—*
> *In the midst of Blue Thunder am I walking—*
> *Now to the straight lightning would I go.*
> *Along the trail that the Rainbow covers—*
> *For to the Big Snake, and to the Blue Thunder*
> *Have I made offering—*
> *Around me falls the white rain,*
> *And pleasant again will all become!"*

Bits, fragments, dragged from the depths of memory by some power—perhaps borrowed from this Drummer. No true Song, just as Hosteen was no true Singer, yet those words stirred the power where it lay coiled deep in his body—or his mind.

Hosteen blinked. The maze of colors that had rippled before his eyes was gone. He fronted an alien face with round skull-set eyes. Only for a moment was there a flicker in those eyes, a belief or an emotion or a thought that matched what Hosteen felt. Then it was gone, and Hosteen was only a Terran settler fitting his hands to those of a Norbie medicine man. The hands drew away from his.

"This one wears the name of Ukurti. You are one who can also summon clouds—younger brother."

"Not so." Hosteen disclaimed any wizard powers. "But on my world, and long ago, my grandfather was such a one. Perhaps he laid upon me something of his own at his passing—"

Ukurti nodded. "That is as it should be, for it is a burden laid upon us who have the strength to pass it to those who can bear it well in their own time. Now there are other matters—this one who has taken the airways into the medicine country rashly and against the laws of your people and mine. This, too, is a part of your burden, younger brother."

Hosteen bowed his head. "This burden do I accept, for it is partly by my doing that he came into this country, and his rashness and evil are as mine."

"That one has gone in—he will not return." Krotag's gestures were emphatic, but he eyed Hosteen with a mixtures of wonder and exasperation.

"That is not for our deciding," corrected Ukurti. "If he is found, you, my younger brother, must deal with him—that we lay upon you."

"That do I accept—"

There was a crackle of sound, not from without but from the mike before Logan. He jerked it up to mouth level.

"Come in—come in!"

"TRI calling base camp—"

Hosteen leaped across the tent and tore the mike from Logan's grasp.

"Storm here—come in TRI—"

"—sighted the LB. Going down for look—on side of mountain—" The din of static half drowned out the words.

Hosteen made an urgent hand signal to Logan and watched his brother snap on the locater. If Widders kept talking, that ought to give them a fix on the present position of the 'copter.

"LB all right—going down!"

"Widders—Widders, wait!" But Hosteen knew that his protest would never be heeded by the men out there. Logan's fingers relayed the information to the Norbies.

"So he has found what he has sought," the Drummer replied. "It may be that his quest wins the favor of the High Dwellers after all. We shall wait and see—"

Hosteen clung to the mike, calling at intervals, but without raising a reply—until, at last, it came with forceful clarity.

"We are going to look for evidence of any survivors. Forgee—Forgee!" The voice grew as shrill as a Norbie pipe, carrying a note of surprise that deepened to alarm. "No! Fire—fire down the mountain. Forgee—they're coming—Storm! Storm!"

"Here!" Hosteen tried to imagine what was happening out there.

"Fire at 'em, Forgee. Got that one!"

"Widders! Are you under attack?"

"Storm—we can't hold 'em off—the fire's spreading too

close. We're going to make a run for it—can hold out in the cave—"

"Hold out against what?" There was no answer from the mike.

"Those-Who-Drum-Thunder have answered," Krotag signed. "This is the end of the evil doer."

"Not so. They may still be alive," Hosteen protested. "We can't leave them there—like that—"

"It has been decided." Krotag's reply was final.

"You," Hosteen appealed to Ukurti, "have said this man is my burden. I cannot leave him there—without knowing the truth of what has happened to him—"

Again it was as if the two of them stood apart from space and time in some emptiness that held only Norbie medicine man and human—that they were in contact in a way Hosteen could never explain.

"The truth was spoken—the burden is yours, and you are not yet loosened from it. These off-worlders have no part of what lies in the Blue, and they have been punished. But I do not think that the pattern is yet finished. The road lies before you; take it without hindrance—"

"If my brother walks this road, then do I also," Logan's hands flashed.

Ukurti turned on the younger man the measuring regard of his paint-ringed eyes. "It is said rightly that brother should shoulder brother when the arrows of war are on the bow string. If this is your choice, let this road be yours also and no one—save the High Dwellers—shall deny it to you."

"This is spoken on the drum?" Using finger speech, Krotag asked Ukurti.

"It is spoken on and by the drum. Let them journey

forth and do what is set upon them. No one can read the path of his beyond-travel. This is a thing to be done." His fingers tapped a small patter of notes on the drum head, a rhythm that sent a crawling chill up Hosteen's back.

From the dark beyond the doorway came Surra, slinking belly to earth, her eyes slitted, her ears tight to her skull. And behind her, Baku, her beak snapping with rage—or some other strong emotion. Last of all Gorgol, stalking like a sleep walker, his eyes staring wide before him. The Drummer gave a last tap and broke the spell.

"Go—you all have been chosen and summoned. Upon you the burden."

"Upon us the burden," Hosteen agreed for all that strangely assorted group of rescuers.

EIGHT

"Mirage?" Logan asked dazedly, perhaps not of his gaunt, hard-driven companions but of the very world about them.

Having won through the cauldron of rocky defiles on foot, for the way they had come was not for horses, it was indeed hard to believe in this valley—the land sloping gently before them, widening out in the distance until they could no longer see the wall heights that guarded it to the west because here the yellow and yellow-green vegetation of the river lowlands was lush. There was no sign of the searing Big Dry cutting down grass and bush. And in the distance there was the shimmer of water—either a curve of river or a lake of some size.

Gorgol braced himself on his folded arms and surveyed the countryside with an expression of awe, while Hosteen sat up, his back against a rock wall still warm enough to feel through his shirt, though this was twilight. Three, four, five days they had spent in hiding, the nights in winning through to this point, where the Blue was at last open before them.

And on the last night only Gorgol's knowledge of the outback had saved them. All water gone, the Norbie had searched the ground on hands and knees, literally smelling out a clue, until he scooped the soil from a small depression. He buried there a hollowed reed with a twist of dried grass about its tip, sucking at the other end with an effort that left him gasping, until after a half hour of such labor he brought liquid up from the source he alone suspected.

Surra whined, nudged against Hosteen, her nostrils expanding as she took in the scents arising from this oasis of the wild. At least to the cat, this was no hallucination, and Hosteen was willing to rely upon her senses sooner than upon his own. Gorgol opened a small pouch on his warrior belt and brought out a pencil-shaped object. He pressed it against one finger tip to leave a small dot of glowing green. Then he drew marks crisscross on his hollow cheeks, in no pattern Hosteen could see, that glowed, making of half his face a weird mask. He held the crayon out to the Terran.

"We go in peace, so this we must do—"

"For the wild men?"

"Not so. For them we must continue to watch. But for Those-Who-Drum, now we bear the marks of peace in their sight."

Hosteen took the soft stick, applied to his own skin a netting of lines, and passed it along to Logan. To every race their customs, and he was willing to follow Gorgol's lead here. The paste on his face stung a little and left the skin feeling drawn and tight.

Although they were now painted for peace, they entered the valley with the caution of raiders. Hosteen guessed that in spite of peace poles passed between age-old enemies, Gorgol's distrust of the wild and rumored cannibal tribes, whose hunting territory this was, still guided his actions.

Baku had flown ahead to the water. Surra padded down the slope before them, blending, in the twilight, with the vegetation, until Hosteen could only follow her movements when she chose to establish mind contact with him. The cat was alert and wary, though she had found nothing suspicious. Now the men followed her, keeping to cover as much as possible.

If there was native life in this valley, it would locate not too far from the water. Yet, water they themselves must have and soon. The heat clung on the upper slope, harsh on their parched bodies. Then Hosteen noted that Gorgol was catching at the headed stems of tall grass, crushing them in his hands and holding the resultant mass to his lips, chewing, spitting. The Terran followed the Norbie's example. He discovered the moisture so gained was a bitter juice, but it eased the dryness of his mouth.

As they went, he looked about them, trying to guess which of the mountains within sight could be that on which Widders had located the LB. The fix from the camp com had guided them here—but now they would have to find the actual wreckage—

Hosteen tensed. His hand went up in a gesture to freeze both of his companions. Surra had given warning. Between them and the water were strange natives. The three flattened against the ground, and now the Terran regretted the luminous paint on their faces, which might be a source of betrayal.

So far, the others did not suspect their presence. Surra

stalked them as they moved steadily along to the south. Hosteen made contact with Baku and knew that the eagle, in turn, would pick up the enemy party.

There were small night sounds. The creatures of the tall grass had not yet gone into Dry Time burrows. Their squeakings and chirpings were loud in Hosteen's ears when he lay on the ground, acutely aware of every small noise, every movement of bush or grass clump. But this was the old, old game the Terran had played so many times during the war years when eyes, noses, keener natural senses than his own, had formed the scouting team, he being the director of activities.

Now, the party of natives had been trailed out of range. The three again had an open path to the water. Hosteen's signal sent them skulking from one piece of cover to the next, working their way through the steadily increasing gloom to the lake—for lake was what Baku reported that body of water to be.

They arrived at the edge of growth of reeds and endured silent torment when insects closed in in a stinging, biting fog. But it was worth that painful, slow progress through mud and slime-coated growing things to plunge their hands into water, scoop up the warm, odorous, and oddly tasting liquid, not only to drink but also to freshen their dehydrated and peeling skins.

Revived, they shared the sustenance tablets brought for emergency rations.

"That mountain—" Logan said. "We'll have to find the right one."

"It is there." To their surprise Gorgol finished his signs with an assured point to the north. "Medicine—and the fire—" But he did not explain that.

Hosteen remembered the night when he had stood in the yard of the Peak holding and watched that flash of light to the north, the flash that had been accompanied by the vibration in the air. That seemed like a long time ago now, and he was visited by an odd reluctance to set out for the mountain Gorgol had set as their goal.

Filling their canteens, they left the lapping waters of the lake, continuing around its perimeter, with Baku aloft in the bowl of the night sky and Surra ranging in a wide pattern back and forth across the line of their advance.

Twice more they took cover to escape Norbie parties. And it was in the last quarter of the night that they began to climb. Bulking big before them so that it cut away the stars was a mountain.

Sound came, first as a faint thumping, then in an ever increasing roll. Drums! Drums with the same compelling power as the small one Ukurti had carried but with far greater range. Logan came up level with Hosteen.

"Village—" He raised his voice to be heard over that roll.

Eastward, Hosteen believed. And he trusted that the drums meant some ceremony was in progress, a ceremony that would keep the villagers safely occupied at home for the few precious hours remaining of the sheltering night.

Surra located the 'copter, her report bringing them to the flattened area of burned-over ground in which lay the twisted, fire-warped framework of the off-world flyer. And not too far away was the half-charred body of the pilot, a burned stump of arrow still protruding from between his shoulders.

"We haven't much time until daybreak. Widders spoke of a cave. We'll separate and look for that," Hosteen said.

Together with Surra, they fanned out from the burned ground upslope. Long line of vegetation ash ridged that rise, puzzling Hosteen by the uniformity of their width and the straight thrust of their lengths. It was almost as if an off-world flamer had been used here—

The Xik? Another holdout group hidden in this remote and forbidden land, just as that other had been when he and Logan had stumbled into their secret base? Those Xiks had used a flamer in their all-out attempt to get Logan when he escaped, destroying their stolen horse herd recklessly in the hope of finishing off one man who could blow wide open their concealed operations on this frontier world. Yes, it was conceivable that another Xik Commando force could be holed up here.

The flamed furrow came to an end abruptly. Here was blackened earth, vegetation charred into powder, and there normal grass, a bush standing high, swaying a little in the predawn wind. Had the flames been aimed up from below, then? But Hosteen had passed nothing in a direct line with the destroyed 'copter and these fire scores that could have produced them. If it wasn't a flamer—then what? Hosteen skirted a bush and began again his hunt for any cave opening, though half mechanically, his mind still partly occupied with the riddle of the fire.

An eye-searing flash lashed the ground only yards ahead, and he stumbled back as flames crackled and bushes flared into torches in the night. Another breakout of the same fire to his left sent Hosteen south and east, running with the fire licking at his heels. He had never seen anything like this before, but the certainty grew, as he fled before the reach of the long red tongues, that the blazes were being used with a purpose, and that purpose— In spite of the heat waves at his back, a chill held the Terran. He was being herded! Someone or something was using a whip of fire to drive him, just as a plains rider used a stock whip to control a stray from the frawn herd.

He stumbled on, striving to pick a way over the now well-lighted ground to avoid any misstep that would leave him the helpless prey of the rage behind him. A small gorge opened ahead, and the Terran made a running leap to cross it, coming down in a panting heap on the far side. When he would have struggled to his feet once more, an arrow quivered deep in the earth by his right hand in blunt warning.

Hosteen hunched together, drawing his feet under him, preparing to spring for freedom if he saw a chance. A ring had closed about him, not of fire but of natives. Unlike the Norbies of the lowlands, these warriors were shorter, closer to Terran build. Their horns were charcoal-black arcs over their skulls, and the same black had been used to draw designs on their faces, not with the aimless crisscross lines that Gorgol had used for peace paint but in intricate and careful patterns.

If he had had a chance in those first few seconds for an attempt at defense or escape, he had lost it now. Whirling out of the flickering half light came one of the native hunters' most effective weapons—a cord net made of the tough, under-the-surface roots of the yassa plant, soaked in water until the mesh was greasy slick. Once enmeshed in that, even a fighting yoris was helpless, as helpless as Hosteen Storm at this moment.

Ignominiously packaged, he was transported downslope to a village, a village that was no collection of skin-covered tents, like those of the nomad Norbies he had known, but of permanent erections with heavy logs rolled shoulder high to form walls, above them a woven wattle of dried vine and reed, with high-peaked thatched roofs.

Out of nowhere had come a Drummer, a medicine man wearing a feather tunic and cloak but in a vivid metallic green, the tunic crossed on the breast with a zigzag, sharp-angled strip of red. And the drum he thumped, as he led the procession carrying the prisoner through the village, was also red. Torches were set up along the way, their flames burning a strange, pale blue. Then Hosteen was out of the open, staring up into the shadows of one of the peaked roofs, as he was dumped roughly on a beaten earth floor.

House—or was it more temple? He tried to assess the meaning of what he saw. There were no sleep rolls in evidence, but in the center of the one huge room was a pit in which burned a fire of the same blue as the torches. And there were cords passing from one to another of the heavy support timber columns the length of the building, lines on which hung bark and shriveled things, together with round objects—

A Thunder House! And those were raid trophies—the heads and hands of dead enemies! Hosteen had heard of that practice as being usual among the Nitra clans. But this building was larger, older, far more permanent than any Nitra wizard tent. The Terran tried to remember every scrap of information he had been able to garner about the Nitra and to apply it to what he could see about him now.

Those warriors who had brought him in were settling down about the fire pit, passing from one to the other a bowl that probably held the mildly intoxicating clava juice, and they showed signs of staying for some hours to come.

The clan Drummer had taken his place on the stool to the north, keeping up a little deep, grumbling sound on his knee drum. That, too, followed the custom of the outer-world tribes—the northern stool for him who drums for the Thunder Ones; the southern stool, still vacant here, for the head Chief of the village or clan.

Hosteen closed his eyes, fixed mind and will on contact with the team, but to no avail. There was nothing—no trace of Surra or Baku—along the mental lanes. He had never quite been able to gauge the range to which his silent command call could reach in relation to either eagle or cat. But this present silence was more than worrying. It carried with it an element of real fear. A man who depended heavily upon the support of a cane could fall helplessly when that cane was snatched from his hand.

The Terran swallowed, as if he could swallow down his rising uneasiness. Had he, through the years, become so wholly identified with the team, so dependent upon them, that he would be a cripple when they did not answer his call? That thought bit deep, so deep he was hardly aware of the Thunder House and those in it until a commotion by the door made him open his eyes and turn his head as well as he could in the confines of the net.

Another party of natives brought a second prisoner, and the Drummer now beat out a heavy tattoo that needed no translation, so filled with triumph was its sound. A minute later the tangled and still struggling captive was dumped beside Hosteen, the lines of his net made fast to the same pillars that held the Terran.

"Hosteen!"

He could barely make out Logan's features, marked still with smears of the luminous paint.

"Here. Gorgol with you?"

"No, haven't seen him since we split up. There was a fire all around, and I blasted out ahead of that. Ran right into this net—they had it strung up waiting between two trees."

Organization, Hosteen granted them that, very efficient organization. Did they have Widders stowed away somewhere here, too? And what was the purpose of their mountain firetrap? Just to capture anyone trying to get up in the heights?

"One thing." Logan broke through the other's mental speculation. "Just before that brush fire walled me off, I saw it."

"It?"

"The LB—it must have been the LB. And from the look I had, it didn't crash when it landed—at least it wasn't smashed up any to show."

"You didn't get a chance to examine it closely though?"

"No," Logan admitted. "Something else queer—"

"That being?"

"There was stuff piled all around it—spears, bowls, hides. And somebody had killed a horse, left it lying with its throat cut and its skull bashed in, right up against the boat— Not too long ago, either."

"Sacrifices."

"Could be. Because the LB came out of the sky, d'you suppose? They can't have seen space ships back here."

"Maybe—but then why attack the 'copter when it came in for a landing," countered the Terran. "If they had no experience with sky craft, one kind could be classed with the other. Unless—"

Unless, his mind raced, they did know the difference between an object from space and one merely traversing Arzoran skies.

"They could have contact with the plains, know the difference between flyers and space ships." Logan was thinking in the same direction.

Or, Hosteen's suspicions suggested, they could have contact with spacers. The fire weapon still posed a puzzle past his present ability to solve.

"This is a Thunder House." Logan had been surveying his surroundings.

"I noticed some similarities with Nitra customs," Hosteen returned. "See anything you know?"

Logan was the expert on native Arzor. Perhaps he could pick up some clue to their future or their captors' intentions. Norbie clans were fond of ritual and tied by custom. There could be a pattern here that would fit with what Logan knew.

"They keep some Nitra ways," his half-brother agreed. "The two stools, north and south, the east and west doors. And—watch that hunter coming in. See how he walks in and out among the pillars and not in a straight line? To do that would mean he was boasting before the powers. Their Drummer, he's going into action now— watch!"

In the eerie light of the blue fire, the Drummer was still pounding his knee drum with two fingers, keeping up a barely audible tap of sound. With the other hand, he had tossed into the air above the fire pit two small white things that floated and soared upward on a puff of the warmer air until they were lost in the gloom of the roof.

"Prayer feathers—or rather fluff," Logan explained. "Those warrior trophies are the same as Nitra, too." He regarded with wry distaste the display of dried hands and skulls. "That's the same way the blue horns hang them—"

"But does the Nitra Drummer do that?" demanded Hosteen sharply.

The medicine man had risen from his stool and put down his drum. Now he stood by the fire, the gaze of all the seated natives centered upon him. From the neck folds of his tunic he pulled a cord from which hung a tube some twelve inches long. It glistened not only with the reflection of the fire but also seemingly with a radiance of its own.

With ceremony the Drummer pointed this to the four points of the compass beginning at the north. And then he aimed one end directly at the air over the fire pit.

A fine spray spread from the end of the tube, carrying glittering, jeweled motes into the air. The motes gathered and formed an outline composed of tiny, spinning gems.

"A five point-star!" Logan cried out.

But already the design was changing, the motes spinning, reforming, this time into a triangle, and then a circle, and finally a shaft that plunged straight down into the fire pit and was gone.

"No Nitra does that!" Logan breathed.

"Nor a Norbie either," Hosteen replied grimly. "That's an off-world thing, of a kind I have never seen before. But I'll take blood oath it isn't native to Arzor!"

"Xik?" Logan demanded.

"I don't know. But I have a suspicion it won't be long before we find out."

NINE

Hosteen tried to flex cramped muscles within the cocoon of net that held him. The night was gone, and none of their captors had so much as come into the quarter of the Thunder House where he and Logan were tethered. Yes—the night was gone.

Daylight struck in places through the thatch and walls of the upper part of the medicine house, but the heat was no greater than it would have been in grazing season on the plains. Within the valley, the Big Dry did not exist at all!

"Sun—but no heat—" he heard Logan mumble. "That lake—"

"Couldn't control the weather," Hosteen countered. They had rivers on the plains, sources of water that did not fail, yet there living things still must take cover during the day.

"Something does," Logan returned obstinately.

Something did. What could control weather? There was one place on—or rather in—Arzor where there was controlled weather and controlled vegetation—the garden mountain into which Logan and Hosteen had blundered on their flight from the Xik—where the Sealed Cave people had set out growing things from a hundred different planets and left them to flourish for centuries. Controlled weather—that was not Xik, that was Sealed Cave knowledge!

"The Sealed Caves—" Hosteen repeated aloud.

"But this is in the open, not in a cave!" Logan's thoughts matched with his. "How could they control the open?"

"How did they fashion that cavern?" Hosteen asked. "But if there are more remains of that civilization here, it could explain a lot."

"The 'medicine,' you mean?"

"Yes, and maybe those tricky air currents that have defeated Survey exploration in here."

"But the Norbies have always avoided the Sealed Caves."

"In the outer Peaks they have, but here we can't be sure the same taboo holds. We can't even be sure that somewhere on Arzor, it might be right here, the Old Ones themselves don't exist still. Don't the legends say that they retired to some of the caves and sealed the openings behind them—eventually to issue forth again in the future?"

Hosteen did not quite believe that, though. That some wild Norbies were exploiting Sealed Cave knowledge—that was possible. That the mysterious and long-gone forerace among the stars could linger on here directing the activities of a primitive tribe or tribes—no, somehow that did not fit. The men, or creatures, who had designed and created the Cavern of the Hundred Gardens could have nothing in common with warriors who kept skulls and right hands of their defeated enemies to adorn their temples. There was a contradiction in mental processes there.

Again Logan's thoughts followed the same path. "I'd rather believe the Norbies were heirs," he said slowly.

"Unworthy ones, I think. Maybe the answer lies on that mountain."

"We'll probably never get a chance to learn it," Logan's reply was bleak. "I think we were cut out of the herd to supply some spectacular touches to a big Drum Feast."

Hosteen had long ago reached the same conclusion. And his struggles against his bonds had proved to him the folly of trying to beat the Norbie system of confining prisoners. One could only fall back on the rather grim thought that as long as one was still alive, there was a small measure of hope.

"Listen!" Logan's head bobbed up as he tried vainly to raise himself a few inches from the floor.

Drums were sounding, more than one now, with a pause between each roll. Hosteen, listening intently, thought he could distinguish a slightly different note in each one of those short bursts.

Norbies had been in and out of the Thunder House all morning, but now a large party entered from the south. Then came a thin, wiry native, his black horns tipped with red, a shoulder plate necklace, not of yoris teeth but of small and well polished bones, covering most of his chest. He took the Chief's stool.

Hosteen's view of the scene was from floor level, but he sighted the second party entering from the west, a peace pole held up ostentatiously. Drummer and Chief walked behind that. When a second and then a third such delegation arrived through the western door, Hosteen realized this was not a gathering of a clan but a meeting of tribal representatives, and from tribes once enemies.

Five, six such delegations now, a handful of warriors ranked behind each chief and medicine man. The seventh—Hosteen started—Krotag and Ukurti led that.

The Drummer of the village was at the north stool. Now he beat a thunderous roll on his knee drum, and two youths broke from the villagers' group, brought out between them a block of wood, square, polished with the sheen of years', perhaps of centuries, handling. Planting this before the fire pit to the north, they laid upon it a leafy branch of the sacred fal tree, then scuttled back to the anonymity of the shadows behind their Drummer.

"Speeches now," Logan half whispered in a lull of drumming.

Speeches there were, and Hosteen longed for the power to translate that whistling-twittering. In turn, the village Drummer and the Chief arose, walked to the block, struck it across the top with the fal branch, and launched into a burst of oratory, from time to time striking the block again with the fal wand to emphasize some point. Then each of the visiting chiefs and drummers followed their example.

Hosteen's head ached, his mouth was parched and dry, and he lay gasping, hardly conscious of the continuing drone at the center of the Thunder House. He wanted water and food—but more than anything, water. Twice he tried to reach Baku, Surra—to no avail. The cat and the eagle might have escaped out of the valley, and he began to hope that they had.

Any chance he and Logan might have had now diminished to the vanishing point. He had thought of Krotag and the Shosonna as possible allies. But Krotag had been the second one to make a speech. Whatever tied the Norbies together in this peace pact was strong enough to withstand any leanings toward friendship with settlers that the plains natives might have once had.

How long that conference lasted neither Hosteen nor Logan could have told. The former was afterwards sure he had lapsed into semiconsciousness from fatigue, lack of water, and the smoky fumes of the fal twigs the Norbies kept feeding into the fire. When a sharp prod in the ribs roused him into full wakefulness, all traces of sunlight were gone and the gloom of night was cut again by blue torches.

One of the same youths who had dragged out the speech block leaned over him and thrust a tube through the mesh of the net and between the Terran's lips. He sucked avidly, and liquid filled his mouth. If it was water, some other substance had been added, for it tasted sweet and yet sharp, like an off-world relish, and Hosteen sucked and swallowed greedily, his thirst vanishing, his mental torpor fading as he did so. Then the tube was jerked roughly from his lips, and he licked them for the last lingering drop, feeling energy creep back into his body. Logan was similarly fed and watered. Beyond the captives stood both the village Chief and the Drummer, watching the process with an air of impatience, as if eager to push on to some more important task.

A ripple of fingers on drum head brought in a guard of

warriors, tough, seasoned fighting men, Hosteen judged from their attitude and the bone necklets they wore. Once more the ropes holding the nets were loosed, and the prisoners, still helpless in their lashings, were rolled like bales into the full torchlight.

Another warrior came out of the shadows, bearing across his shoulder the loops of their arms belts, their canteens. It would seem that where they were going their equipment was to accompany them. And for the first time, Hosteen remembered Logan's grisly description of what he had seen about the grounded LB—sacrifices. Were they about to join the horse, to do honor to whatever power these Norbies imagined the star ship escape craft represented or held?

They had been carried into the village, but they were to walk out. Nets were whirled off their stiff bodies, a loop rope dragged tight about their chests and upper arms. Hosteen stumbled along for a step or two, trying to make his cramped limbs obey. Then two of his captors caught him by the shoulder on either side as supports and herders.

For the first time he saw the females of the village well behind the lines of warriors. Yes, some ceremony was in prospect, one intended for all the tribesmen and their visitors—for under each peace pole, which they had seen in the Thunder House earlier and which now were planted here in the open, was a grouping of strangers.

The two men were half led, half dragged along a well-worn trail leading from the village toward the dark bulk of the mountainside down which the fire had hunted them into their captors' nets. Behind, as Hosteen saw when he glanced back once, trying to pick out Krotag's group, the villagers and their guests fell in to form a straggling procession, carrying torches.

As they advanced, the smell of burned vegetation battled with that of fal wood. And they crossed those curiously straight furrows where the flails of flame must have beaten, either during their own chase or earlier.

Now the drums were beating. Not only that of the village medicine man but also those of all the visiting Drummers—with a heavy rhythm into which their marching steps fitted. And the beat of the drums became one with Hosteen's pumping blood, a heaviness in his head—

Hypnotic! Hosteen recognized the danger. His own people could produce—or had produced ages ago—spells as a part of their war chants and dances, spells to send men out to kill with a firm belief in the invincibility of their "medicine." This was not a pattern unique to Arzor.

He tried a misstep to break the pattern of the march. And perhaps because he had been indoctrinated during his Service training against just such traps, the Terran succeeded in part—or was succeeding—until the mountain came alive in answer to those with whom he marched.

That was what appeared to happen. Was it sound—vibration pitched too high or too low for human ears to register except on the very border of the senses? Or was it mental rather than physical? But it was as if all the bulk of earth and rock exhaled, breathed, stirred into watchful wakefulness. And Hosteen knew that this was something totally beyond his experience, perhaps beyond the experience of any off-worlder—unless Widders had met this before him.

Beat, beat—in spite of his efforts of mind, will, and

squirming body held tight in the vice grip of the warriors who marched with him—Hosteen could only resist that enchantment feebly. That he was able to recognize and fight it at all was, he thought, a slender defense. Beat, beat—feet, drums— And again the mountain sighed— sighed or drew in a breath of anticipation—which? This was no earth and rock but a beast crouched there waiting, such a beast as no human could imagine.

The stench of the burned stuff was stronger. Then there was a last crescendo from the united drums—a roll of artificial thunder echoing and reechoing from the heights. They stopped and stood where they were, facing upslope toward the unseen top of the mountain. Then, as the drums had acted as one, so did the torch bearers move, stamping their lights into the earth, leaving them all in the dark, with only the far stars pricking the cloudless sky.

There was not a sound as the last echoes of the drumbeats died. Would the beast who was the mountain make answer? Hosteen's imagination presented him with a picture of that creature—sky-high—waiting— Waiting as Surra could wait, as Baku could wait, with the great patience that man has lost or never had, the patience of the hunter.

The waiting Norbies—the waiting mountain—and waiting prisoners—

Again that breath, that sound that could not be heard, only felt with each atom of his tense body.

Then—

Lightning—great, jagged, broken blades of lightning stabbing up into the sky, lighting the slope. It played about the round knob that Hosteen saw for the first time clearly as the crest of the mountain—knob, one part of mind remaining undazzled told him, that was too round to be natural. A crown of lightning about the rock head of a crouching beast. Then—the whips of blazing light cracked down, cut and fired, and the smoke of those fires carried to the waiting throng. Crack, lash—but behind that was no natural force but intelligent purpose. Hosteen was sure of that as he stood blinded by the flashes.

Xik—this could not be Xik. The installations that must govern this display were no Xik flamers, nor anything he had seen or heard of on other worlds. Yet Hosteen's mind balked at associating this weapon for horrible destruction with the same civilization that had produced the beauty of the Cavern of the Hundred Gardens.

As swiftly as it had begun, it was over. Brush was in flames at widely separated places on the upper slopes, but the fires did not spread far. And now the drums began once again their marching tap. Hosteen's guards pushed him ahead. However, this time the bulk of the villagers remained where they were, only the local Chief, his guards, the Drummer, and their captives climbed anew.

Once more they passed the burned frame of the 'copter. The recent fiery lashes must have struck it again, for the tail assemblage was now a molten mass, glowing as the metal slowly cooled. Past the 'copter—on and up—

Gorgol, Surra, Baku—had they somehow escaped both the nets of the natives and the lightning? Hosteen tried to call again, only to meet that curious deadness in response, as if there had never been any way he could communicate with those intelligent brains so different from his own.

"LB just ahead," Logan called out.

Hosteen sniffed the sickly sweet smell of decay—decay

of vegetable and animal matter—the sacrifices, if sacrifices they were meant to be. And were he and Logan now being taken to join those? The Terran knew a trick or two he could use at the last, even with his arms bound—

The slaughtered horse was visible in the flicker of a dying brush fire, behind it the shape of the LB. And as Logan had reported, there were no signs of a fatal crash landing. The escape boat might have been set down as easily as if it landed on the mountainside by directing radar. Survivors? Or had the survivors already gone the path he and Logan were traveling?

Hosteen so expected a battle at the site of the LB that he was startled when they did not pause there. The Drummer tapped, blew a puff of the prayer fluff in the direction of the craft, but they did not approach it.

No—the mountain was still waiting. And again in Hosteen's imagination it took on the semblance of a slightly somnolent yet watchful animal—yet an animal with a form of intelligence.

Up again—and now the slope was steeper, rougher, so that Hosteen and Logan were hauled and dragged by their guards' ropes, struggling to keep their feet at times. Once Hosteen went to his knees and refused to respond to the tugging, striving to combine his need for a breathing spell with the chance for a look about.

Since they had left the LB, they had crossed several of the burned furrows, but these were of an earlier date, since they did not smoke. And now more and more rocky outcrops broke through the vegetation carpeting the slopes. The brush was left behind, and they were surrounded by rock. There was a narrow cleft where they felt their way up a niche stair, the prisoners scraped along painfully by their guards.

The cleft brought them to a ledge almost wide enough to be termed a small plateau. In the rock of the cliff that backed it was a dark opening. But this was not their goal, for the party struck eastward to the right, following the width of ledge around a gentle curve Hosteen judged to be the base of the mountain's dome crest, though that must still climb some hundreds of feet above.

Daylight was coming, and he hoped the strange immunity that protected the village and the valley held here, too—that they need not fear the rising of the sun. Or was that to furnish the manner of their ending, death by exposure to the fury of its rays on a sacred mountain?

Already they were out of sight of the cave opening, and here the ledge extended from curving cliff wall to an edge that overhung a frightening drop to unguessed depths. The smooth path under his boots reminded Hosteen of another mountain road that had appeared to run from nowhere in the heights at the mountain of the Garden. That had been a relic of the Sealed Cave civilization, and on it Hosteen had nearly met death in the person of the Xik aper, the last of his breed on Arzor.

The ledge road ended as if sheared off by giant knife stroke. To their left was the circle of another doorway into the cliff wall—but this was sealed by what appeared a smooth slate of rock. The Drummer sounded his ritual signal—perhaps in salute to whatever power he deemed lurked behind that barrier.

And when the echo of that died away, the Chief of the village took the captives' arms belts from the guard. With deliberation he broke the blades of their long hunting knives and showed his familiarity with the use of stunners by crushing their barrels with a rock ax the Drummer produced. Having destroyed the outlanders' weapons, he whistled, and two of the guards went into action.

Planting palms flat against the surface of the closed door, they exerted full strength, straining muscles on arms and shoulders.

The barrier gave, split vertically apart. Into that opening the Chief tossed the ruined weapons, the belts of the prisoners. And then the two captives were thrust forward with such force that they hurtled helplessly into a thick dark against which the light of day at their backs made little impression.

TEN

Hosteen brought up against an unseen wall with force enough to bruise flesh, to drive breath out of his body in a gasping grunt. He was on his knees, trying to regain both breath and balance when Logan crashed into him, and they both went to the rock surface under them. There was absolute darkness now. The Norbies must have resealed the cave.

The Terran knew of old that particular type of airlessness, that dead feeling—it was found in the passages of the Sealed Caves, long closed to man, perhaps always intended to be closed to his species. This was certainly a relic of the Sealed Cave civilization.

Breathing shallowly, he lay still and tried to think.

"One of the old caves," Logan broke silence first. "It smells like one anyway—"

"Yes."

"Any chance of getting loose?"

Hosteen, moving his arms, was rewarded by a slight give of his bonds.

"Might be." He continued his efforts.

"Ha!" That was an exclamation of triumph from Logan. "That does it! Here—where are you?"

A hand, moving through the thick blanket of no light, clutched at Hosteen's shoulder and moved swiftly down to the coils of rope about him.

"They weren't very clever with their knots." Logan's fingers were now busy behind Hosteen's back.

"I don't think"—the Terran sat up, massaged his right wrist with the fingers of his left hand—"we were meant to stay tied or they would have left the nets on us. Now—let's just see—"

He had no idea how big the cave was or how far they were from the outer door. Nor was he too sure in which direction that door lay. The odd quality of this dark and the lifeless feel of the air did weird things to alter a man's sense of direction—even, Hosteen suspected, influenced his clarity of thought. He stood for a long second or two, trying to orientate himself before he moved in a shuffle, half crouched, to sweep the floor with one hand, while the other was out before him as insurance against coming up short against another wall.

"Stay right where you are," he ordered Logan.

"What's the game?"

"They threw our belts in after us, broke our weapons, but I've an atom torch on that belt. And they didn't damage that, at least not while I was watching—"

Sweep—sweep—finger tips scraping on stone, nails gritting—then the smoothness of hide worked into leather! The Terran squatted, drew his find to him, knew by touch it was Logan's, and looped the belt around his shoulder for safe keeping.

117

"Got yours," he reported. "Mine can't be too far away."

Once more sweep—sweep. His fingers were growing tender. Then they rapped against an object, and there was a metallic sound. He was holding a ruined stunner. Only a few inches beyond that—his belt!

Hosteen slipped it hurriedly through his hands, locating radar compass, a pouch of sustenance tablets, the small emergency medical kit, to find in the last loop next to the empty knife sheath the pencil-slim eight-inch tube he was looking for. He pushed its wide fan button and blinked at a blinding answer of light.

"Whew!" Logan's exclamation was tinged with awe.

They were in a cave right enough, and the interior walls and roof had been coated with that same dull black substance they had seen in the passages to the caverns of the gardens, the building material of the unknown star travelers.

In a tangle by the door, now closed so that even the seam of its opening was invisible, were objects that certainly did not date back to the period of the Sealed Caves. Hosteen went to examine the exhibits. Their own broken bladed hunting knives and Logan's smashed stunner lay there, but there were other things—another stunner, another belt, this one heavily weighted with a third again as much equipment as the one he had worn into the Peaks.

Hosteen picked that out of the dust.

"Widders!" He got to his feet and held up the torch so its glow covered as much of the cave as possible. But there was no sign of the civ—if he had preceded them into captivity here.

"Maybe there's another passage here—" Logan drew

his half-brother's attention to a jutting of wall at the left where a shadow might mask an opening. And it did—there was a dark hole there.

Logan gathered up the rope of their bonds and coiled it belt-wise about his waist. They had no weapons—or did they? Hosteen hefted the belt that had belonged to Widders. Knife and stunner were gone from their sheaths, but he remembered the off-world weapon that had subdued them when the civ had started on his mad quest into the Blue. And there was a chance some similar surprise might be part of this equipment.

"Do we go?" Logan stood at the mouth of the tunnel.

Hosteen had located a pouch envelope on Widders' belt. He shook from it into his hand a ball an inch and a half in diameter, with a small knob projecting from its smooth surface. It had the appearance of a small antiperso grenade. He looked from it to the sealed door in speculation. A full-sized antiperso grenade was a key to unlock a piece of field armor, planted in the right way at the right time, and Hosteen had planted them so. What effect would a grenade one third the regular size have on the cave door?

"Find somethin' interestin'?" Logan asked.

"Might just be." Hosteen outlined in a terse sentence or two what he thought he held and its uses.

"Get the door down with that?"

Hosteen shrugged. "I don't know—might be chancy. We don't know the properties of this alien cave-sealing material. Remember what happened that other time?"

Months before, the back lash of an Xik weapon used miles away had reacted violently on the alien coating of just such a cave, locking them into what, except for chance, might have been a living tomb. They had escaped then, but one could not depend on personal "medicine" too long or too hard.

"I say, try the back door first." Logan indicated the passage.

And that made good sense. Widders was not in the cave, and if he had been a prisoner here, he might have taken that way before them. There had been many indications that the Unknowns had been fond of under-mountain ways and were adept at boring them.

They sorted over the equipment, dividing up the grenades, ration tablets, supplies. Water—they had no water save that in the canteens, but at least they were not exposed to the baking sun.

No passage ran beyond that wall. They found instead a steeply sloping, downward ramp where there was no dust to cushion the black flooring. They advanced slowly. Hosteen ahead, the torch in one hand, a sweat-sticky grenade in the other.

The Terran heard Logan sniff as one might scent-danger.

"Water—somewhere ahead."

For a moment Hosteen's imagination painted for him the picture of another pocket paradise like the Cavern of the Hundred Gardens. But where there had been the aromatic odors of clean and spicy things to tantalize them then, here was a dank breath not only of dampness but also of other and even less pleasant smells.

Along the walls the torch picked up beads of moisture, which gave black prismatic flickers of color. Logan ran his finger along to wipe out a cluster, then rubbed it vigorously on the edge of his yoris-hide-corselet with an exclamation of disgust.

"Slime!" He held the finger to his nose. "Stinks, too. I'd say we might be on our way straight down into a drain—"

The drops on the wall coalesced into oily runlets, and the nephritic odor grew stronger. Yet the air was not still. There was a draft rising, bringing with it a fog of corruption.

All the way down they had seen no indication that anyone had come before them. But now they reached a point where there was a huge blotch across the slope of the wall, where the runlets had been smeared together, through which new trickles were now cutting paths. The damp had prevented the drying of the splotch.

"That wasn't done too long ago," Logan observed. He put out his own hand, though he did not touch finger to the wall, to show that the top of the smear was at shoulder height. "Someone or something could have fallen and slipped down there—"

Hosteen swung the torch closer to floor level. Logan's deduction was borne out by still undried marks.

"And that"—Logan pounced upon one of the damp spots—"was the toe of a boot!"

Again his tracker's eye was right. Only the toe of an off-world boot could have left that well-defined curve. Widders? Or some survivor from the LB holding up in this mountain maze against the danger of the natives waiting outside?

"He went down—he did not come back—whoever he was," Logan observed.

"Meaning that he might not have been able to retreat?

Well, we either go on or try to break that door down with a grenade. Have any second thoughts on the matter?"

"Go on." Logan's answer was prompted. "We have stingers in these." He tossed a grenade into the air and caught it deftly.

They went on, watching floor and wall for any further traces of the one or ones who had taken that passage before them, but sighted none. Only the damp increased until the air was half-foggy moisture. And where, in the upper regions, that moisture had been chill, here it was increasingly warm, warm and odorous. There was a musky taint, which set Hosteen to sniffing, hinting of life ahead.

The passage was no longer a steep descent; it was beginning to level off. And now the dripping walls supplied a thin stream of water carried in a depression down the center of the floor, flowing ahead. The torch caught the edge of an archway that led out—out where—into what?

As they went through it, Hosteen switched the beam of the torch from a diffused glow into a single spear point of concentrated light. He thought he could see a shadowy point somewhere far to the right, which could be shoreline or wall. But below was a spread of oily water on which patches of floating stuff turned rainbow-hued when the light caught them, fading into dullness as they moved out of its beam once more.

The passage, which had brought them here, ran on out into the water, as a wharf or pier of rock, obviously artificially fashioned. And along its surface at intervals were rings of the same rock standing on end as if waiting for mooring ropes. Mooring ropes—for what manner of craft? Who had sailed this lake or river and for what purpose?

Together they walked slowly along that wharf—the bare rings, the greasy, ill-smelling flood that washed sluggishly along its side—The Cavern of the Hundred Gardens had been alien—alien but not inimical. Here there was a difference. Again Hosteen could not reconcile the minds that had created the gardens and those that had engineered these borings in the mountain of the Blue.

"What kind of ships?" Logan asked suddenly. "Who were they and why did they want ships here? The Gardens—and this place—don't match."

"They are not the same," Hosteen agreed. "Kwii halchinigii 'ant'iihnii—"

"What?"

"I said—this place smells of witchcraft."

"That is the truth!" Logan commented with feeling. "Where do we go now? Somehow I don't fancy swimmin'."

They had reached the end of the wharf and were gazing out over the sluggishly flowing water, trying to catch some landmark in the beam of the torch. But save for those vague shadows far to the right, there was nothing to suggest this place had any boundaries beyond.

It was when Hosteen swung the torch left to pick out a continuation of the wall through which they had come that they sighted a possible exit. A beach of sorts extended along this side of the cavern—several yards of coarse sand and gravel between the foot of the wall and the lapping of the dark water. And along the wall itself were dark shadows, which might or might not contain the openings to further caves or passages. It was more inviting to investigate than the water, for Hosteen agreed with Logan's comment moments earlier—this was not a place to tempt a swimmer. The very look of that opaque flood suggested unpleasant things lurking below its encrusted surface.

They retreated along the wharf, leaped from it to the fringe of beach. Here and there stones of some size were embedded in the gravel—or were they stones? Hosteen stopped and toed one of them over with his boot. The black eye holes of a skull stared back at him. Curving horns rooted in the bone told him that a Norbie had died here. Some time ago he judged by the condition of the bone.

"In the Name of the Seven Thunders, what's that?" Logan caught at Hosteen's arm, dragged the torch forward. And again its gleam picked out details of bleached bone.

But such bone! Hosteen found it hard to picture that great head ever enclosed in flesh. Half buried in the gravel as the skull now was, the angle of that fanged jaw as long as his arm, the huge pits of eye sockets, were like nothing he had ever seen on Arzor or on fifty other planets either.

"Three eyes!" Logan's voice sounded weirdly over the lisping lap of the water. "It had three eyes!"

He was right. Two eye sockets abnormally far to each side were centered by a third midpoint above the jagged toothed jaw. Three eyes!

On Terra there had been monsters in the far past whose bones had endured out of their own era into the time of humankind, so that man had dug them free of earth and rock and set them up in museums to marvel at.

Perhaps this was one of the ancient things that had once dominated Arzor, its kind long since vanished from the planet. Yet Hosteen did not think so. Those three eye sockets were a distortion, alien.

"It must have been a monster!" Logan was down on his knees scraping at the gravel gingerly, as if he did not want to touch the bone with his bare hands. And now Hosteen surveyed the exposed skull narrowly. He went back, picked up the Norbie one by a horn, and brought it to rest beside that three-eyed thing, comparing one to the other.

"What's the matter?" Logan wanted to know.

"Shil hazheen—"

Logan looked at him in some exasperation. "Talk so a fella can understand, won't you?"

"I am confused," Hosteen obligingly translated. "This is impossible."

"What is?"

"This skull"—Hosteen pointed to the Norbic—"is crumbling away from age, perhaps from damp. Yet it is of a native, a type of Arzoran life that exists today. Compare it with this other one. The three-eye is no different; they could be of the same age—"

"What are you tryin' to say?"

Hosteen spoke of the early giant reptiles on Terra, of the chance that this might have been a relic of pre-intelligent life on Arzor.

"Only it doesn't look old enough—that's what you mean? Well, couldn't the Norbie have been old, too?"

"That might be so—to each planet its own history. Only on Terra such monsters had vanished long before the first primitive man had evolved. And surely Norbie legends would mention these if they had shared the same world at the same time."

"The plains people have always been afraid of the Blue."

"But not for any reason such as monsters, for they do talk of those giant killer birds and every other known natural menace."

"Which means—?"

"That if these things were alive only a short time ago, historically speaking, say a century or so in the past, they might have been confined to underground places such as this, known only to victims trapped here."

"And that some three-eye could be waitin' right around the next bend now?" Logan got to his feet and brushed sand from his hands. "That isn't the most cheerful news in the world?"

"I could be wrong." But Hosteen was not going to relax any vigilance on that count. And how much advantage would an antiperso grenade give him over sudden death watching through three eyes?

They went on down the beach at a slower pace, using the torch on every dark spot before them, alert to any sound. Yet the lap of the water, the crunch of their boots on the coarse gravel was all they heard.

So far none of those shadows had concealed any further openings. But they were well away from the wharf when Logan again caught at Hosteen's touch hand, directing the beam higher on the wall.

"Somethin' moved—up there!"

Out into the path of the light flew a winged creature uttering a small, mewling cry. The light brought into vivid life yellow wings banded with white.

"Feefraw!" Logan named one of the common berry-feeding birds to be found along any mountainside. "But what is it doing in here?"

"It could be showing us a way out." Hosteen aimed his light straight for the spot from which the bird had come. There was an opening deeper than any of the shallow crevices they had discovered so far. The feefraw must have gotten into the mountain somewhere, perhaps down this very passage.

The bird circled around in the path of the beam, and now, as if guided by the light, went back to the hole above, where it settled down on the edge, still mewling mournfully.

"Back door?" Logan suggested.

"No harm in trying it."

An advantage of that hole was that it certainly did not look large enough to accommodate the bulk of any creature with a skull as big as the one they had found. One could travel that road without fearing a monster lurking behind every rock ahead. Hosteen tucked the torch into the front of his shirt and began to climb toward that promising niche.

ELEVEN

They stood together in the opening of another cave. Could they hope by the evidence of the bird that it was the mouth of a passage, a passage giving upon light, air, and the clean outer world?

If this was a passage, it was not a smoothed, coated one, made ready for use by the Unknowns. Here there was no black coating on the walls, only the rough purpled-red of the native stone. But there was a way before them, and as they started, the feefraw cried and fluttered along behind as if drawn by the torch light.

Unhappily the way did not slope upward but ran straight, in some places so narrow that they had to turn sidewise and scrape through between jutting points of rock. But the air was a moving current, and it lacked the strange quality of that in the alien ways.

Logan sniffed again. "Not too good."

It was back, the musky taint that had been strong before they came out into the cavern of the river. Musky taint, and damp—yet Hosteen was sure they had not circled back. They could not have returned to the beach beyond the wharf.

The feefraw had continued to flutter behind. Now its mewling became a mournful wail, and it flew with blind recklessness between the two men and vanished ahead down the passage. Hosteen pushed the pace as they came out into a gray twilight. He snapped off the torch, advanced warily, and looked down onto a scene so weird that for a moment he could almost believe he was caught in a dream nightmare.

They were perched in a rounded pocket in the wall of another cavern—but a cavern with such dimensions that perhaps only an aerial survey could chart it. Here, too, was water—streams, ponds, even a small lake. But the water was housed between walls. The floor of the cavern as far as he could see in the grayish light, was a giant game board. Walled squares enclosed a pond and a small scrap of surrounding land, or land through which a stream wandered. For what purpose? There were no signs of cultivated vegetation such as a farm field might show.

"Pens." Logan's inspiration clicked from possibility to probability.

Those geometrically correct enclosures could be pens—like the home corrals of a holding in the plains. But pens to confine what—and why?

They squatted together trying to note any sign of movement in the nearest enclosures. The vegetation there was coarse, reedy stuff, as pallidly gray as the light, or low-growing plants with thick, unwholesome-looking fleshy leaves. The whole scene was repellent, not enticing as the Cavern of the Hundred Gardens had been.

"This has been here a long time," Logan observed. "Look at that wall there—"

Hosteen sighted on the section Logan indicated. The walls had collapsed, giving access to two other enclosures. Yes, and beyond was another tumbled wall. The pens, if pens they had been, were no longer separated. He stood up and unhooked the distance lenses from his belt. The light was poor, but perhaps he could see what lay beyond their immediate vicinity.

He swept the glasses slowly across the territory from right to left. Pens, water, growing stuff, the same as those that lay below them. There was a difference in the type of vegetation in several places, he thought. And one or two of the enclosures were bare and desertlike, either by design or the failure of the odd "crop" once grown there.

The walls were not the only evidence of once purposeful control, Hosteen discovered, as his distance lenses caught a shadowy pile at the far left. It was a building of some sort, he believed, and said as much to Logan. The other, taking the lenses in turn, confirmed his guess.

"Head for that?" he wanted to know.

It was a logical goal. At the same time, surveying those "pens," Hosteen was aware of a strange reluctance to venture down into the walled squares and oblongs, to force a way through the sickly and sinister-looking growth they held. And Logan put the same squeamishness into words.

"Don't like to trail through that somehow—"

Hosteen took back the glasses and studied the distant building. The murky dusk of the cavern's atmosphere made it somehow unsubstantial when one attempted to pin down a definite line of wall or a roof or even the approximate size of the structure. This was like trying to see clearly an object that lay beyond a misty, water-splashed window. And perhaps that was part of the trouble—the dank air here was not far removed from fog.

There was certainly no sign of any movement about the place, just as there was none in the pens, save the ripple of some wandering stream. Hosteen did not believe that intelligence lingered here, though perhaps other life might. And the building might not only explain the purpose of the cavern but also show them some form of escape. Those who had built this place had surely had another mode of entrance than the narrow, ragged rock fault that had led the settlers in.

"We'll try to reach that." When he voiced those words, Hosteen was surprised at his own dubious tone.

Logan laughed. "Devil-devil country," he commented. "I'd like it better takin' this one with some of our boys backin' our play. Let's hope our long-toothed, three-eyed whatsit isn't sittin' down there easy-like just waitin' for supper to walk within grabbin' range, and me without even a knife to do any protestin' about bein' the main course. Waitin' never made a thing easier though. Shall we blast off for orbit?"

He swung over the lip of the drop with Hosteen following. Their boots thudded into the loose soil as they fell free for the last foot or so and found themselves in one of the walled patches where the barriers were at least ten feet tall. Had it not been for broken areas, they might not have been able to make their way from one pocket to the next, for what remained of the walls was slick-smooth.

Twice they had to form human ladders to win out of pens where the boundaries were still intact. And in one of those they discovered another bony remnant from the past—a skull topping a lace of vertebra and ribs, the whole forming skeletal remains of a creature Hosteen could not identify. There was a long, narrow head with a minute brain pan, the jaws tapering to a point, in the upper portion of which was still socketed a horn, curving up.

Logan caught at that and gave it a twist. It broke loose in his hand, and he held aloft a wicked weapon some ten inches long, sharp as any yoris fang and probably, in its day, even more dangerous.

"Another whatsit."

"Someone was collecting," Hosteen guessed, walking around that rack of bones. He thought that was the reason for the pens—the water. Just as the Cavern of the Hundred Gardens had represented a botanical collection culled from at least a hundred different worlds for their beauty and fragrance, here another collection had been kept—reptiles, animals—who knew? This could have existed as some sort of zoo or perhaps stockyard. Yet where the gardens had flourished over the centuries or eons after the disappearance of the gardeners, this had not.

"We ought to be glad of that," was Logan's quick reply to the Terran's comment. "I don't fancy bein' hunted when I can't do any markin' up in return. This would make a good huntin' trophy." He balanced the horn in his hand, then thrust its point deep into the empty sheath where his knife had once ridden. "Bet Krotag's never seen anythin' like it."

"Those broken walls—" Hosteen sat side by side with his half-brother on the unbreached one of the skeleton enclosure. "Suppose whoever was in charge here left suddenly—"

"And the stock got hungry and decided to do somethin' about it?" Logan asked. "Could be. But just think of things that could smash through somethin' as tough as this!" He slapped his hand on the surface under him. "That would be like seein' a crusher alive, wild, and rarin' to blast! Glad we came late—this would be no place to 'first ship' when that breakout was goin' on."

They kept on their uneven course over walls and through pens. The tablets of emergency rations they had chewed from time to time gave them energy and put off the need for sleep. But Hosteen knew that there was a point past which it was dangerous to depend upon that artificial strength, and they were fast approaching the limit. If they could find refuge in the building ahead, then they could hole up for a space, long enough to get normal rest. Otherwise, the bolstering drug could fail at some crucial moment and send them into helpless collapse.

On top of the last wall they paused again, while Hosteen turned the beam of the torch on the waiting building. Between their present perch and that there was a line of slim, smooth posts set in the earth. But if they had been put there to support a fence, the rest of that barrier had long since disappeared. And as far as the two explorers could see, the way to the wedge-shaped door in the massive two-story structure was open.

Slipping from the wall, they were well out toward those posts when Hosteen halted and flung out an arm quickly to catch at Logan. Memories of safeguards on remote worlds stirred. Because one could not see a barrier was no reason to believe there was none there. If the creatures confined back in the pens had burst through the walls, the keepers of this place must have possessed some form of defense and protection to handle accidents. A force-field now, generated between those poles, he warned. Logan nodded.

"Could be." He caught up a stone and hurled it through the space directly before them. It struck with a sullen clunk on the wall beside the door of the building, passing the pole area without hindrance.

"If it ever was there—it must be gone now."

The evidence was clear, yet a part of Hosteen walked in dread as they advanced. Instinct, rained and tested many times in the past, instinct that was a part of that mysterious inborn gift making him one with the team, argued now against this place. He fought that unease as he stepped between the poles.

His hands went to his ears. He cowered, threw himself forward, and rolled across the hard ground in an agony that filled his head with pain, that was vibration, noise, something alien enough so that he could not put name to it! The world was filled with a piercing screaming, which tore at his body, cell by living cell. Hosteen had known physical pain and mental torment in the past, but nothing had ever reached this point—not in a sane world.

When he was again conscious, he lay in the dark, huddled up, hardly daring to breathe lest that punishment return. Then, at last, he moved stiffly, levered himself up, conscious of light at his back. He looked over his shoulder at a wedge-shaped section of gray. Wedge-shaped! The door in the building! He had reached the building then. But what had happened? He forced himself to remember, though the process hurt.

The pole barrier—a sonic, a sonic of some sort! Logan—Logan had been with him! Where was he now?

Hosteen could not make it to his feet; the first attempt made his head whirl. He crawled on his hands and knees back into the open and found Logan on the ramp that led to the doorway, moaning dully, his eyes closed, his hands to his head.

"What was it?" They lay side by side now within the first room of the building. Logan got out the question in a hoarse croak.

"A sonic, I think."

"That makes sense." Sonics were known to frawn herders, but the devices were not in general good favor. Such broadcasters had to be used by a master and were not easily controlled. The right degree of sound waves could keep a herd in docile submission, a fraction off and you had a frenzied stampede or a panic that could send half your animals to their deaths, completely insane.

"Still working—but it didn't kill us," Logan commented.

"Tuned in for a different life form," Hosteen pointed out. "Might not kill them either—just stun. But I don't want another dose of that."

Their experience of crossing the barrier had wrung the last of their drug-supported strength from them. They slept, roused to swallow tablets and drink from the canteens they had filled at one of the pen springs, and drifted off to sleep again. How long had lethargy lasted they could not afterwards decide. But they awoke at last, clear-headed and with a measure of their normal energy.

Logan studied two sustenance tablets lying on his palm. "I'd like me some real chewin' meat again," he announced. "These things don't help a man forget he's empty—"

"They'll keep us going—"

"Goin' where?"

"There must be some way out of here. We'll just have to find it."

They had explored the building. If the keepers of the pens had left in such a hurry that they had not had time to care for the future of their captive specimens, still they had taken the contents of the rooms with them. No clues remained among those bare walls as to the men or creatures who had once lived here. That the building had been a habitation was proved by a washing place they found in one room and something built into another that Hosteen was sure was a cook unit. But all else was gone, though holes and scars suggested installations ripped free in a hurry.

When they reached the top floor of the building, they found a way out onto the flat roof, and from that vantage point they studied what they could see of the surrounding cavern.

At the back of the structure there were no pens. A smooth stretch of ground led directly to a passage-opening in the cave wall—a very large one.

"That's the front door," Logan observed. "Straight ahead—"

"Straight ahead—but with something in between." Hosteen pivoted, surveying the surrounding terrain. He was right; the posts marking the sonic barrier made a tight, complete circle about the building. To reach the tempting "front door" meant recrossing that unseen barrier. And to do that—

Also, why did he keep thinking that there was a menace lurking out there? The only living thing they had seen in any of these burrows was the feefraw that had somehow

136

found its way into this deserted world. The bones of the creature that had once been penned here were old enough to crumble. Yet whenever he faced those walled squares, his flesh crawled, his instincts warned. There was some danger here, something they had not yet sighted.

"Look!" Logan's hand on his shoulder pulled him around. He was now facing the entrance to the big passage. "There," his half-brother directed, "by that side pillar."

The sides of the passage opening had been squared into pillars, joined to the parent rock. And Logan was right; here was a dark bundle on the ground at the foot of one. Hosteen focused the distance lenses. The half light was deceiving but not enough to conceal the nature of what lay there—that could only be a man.

"Widders?" Logan asked.

"Might be." Had that crumpled figure stirred, tried to raise a hand? If that were Widders and he had crossed the sonic barrier, he could have been knocked out only temporarily.

"Come on," Hosteen called, already on his way from the roof.

"Make it quick," Logan answered.

That could be their best defense—a running leap with impetus enough to tear a man through the beam. Hosteen knew of no other way to cross without the shields they did not possess. Having tested the straps of their equipment, they toed the mark just beside the outer wall, then sprinted for the pole line.

Hosteen launched himself, felt the tearing of the sonic waves as he shot through them, landed beyond, to roll helplessly, battling unconsciousness. Logan spiraled over him with flailing arms and legs and lay now beyond.

Somehow the Terran fought to his knees. It seemed to him the shock this time was less. He crawled to Logan, who was now striving to sit up, his mouth drawn crooked in his effort to control his whisper.

"We made it—"

They crouched together, shoulder touching shoulder, until their heads cleared and they were able to stand. Then they headed for the man by the pillar.

Hosteen recognized the torn coverall. "Widders! Widders!" He wavered forward, to go down again beside the quiet form. Then his eyes fastened on one outflung hand unbelievingly.

Skin over bone, with the bone itself breaking through the tight pull of the skin on the knuckles! Fighting his fear of the dead, the inborn sense of defilement, he took the body by one shoulder, rolled it over on its back—

"No—no!" Logan's cry was one of raw horror.

This thing had been Widders, Hosteen was sure of that. What it was now, what anyone could swear to, was that it might once have been human. The Terran thrust his hands deep into the harshness of the sand, scrubbed them back and forth, wondering if he would ever be able to forget that he had touched this—this—

"What did—that?" Logan's demand was a whisper.

"I don't know." Hosteen stood up, one hand pressed to his heaving middle. His instinct had been right. Somewhere here lurked a hunter—a hunter whose method of feeding was far removed from the sanity of human life. They must get away—out of here—now!

He grabbed for Logan, shoved him toward the passage

Widders must have been trying to reach when he had been pulled down. There was a horror loose in this place that had not died long ago in those pens—if it had ever been confined there.

They ran for the open passage and sped into the dark mouth of the tunnel. And they fled on blindly into that thick dark until there was a band of tight, hard pain about their lower ribs and the panic that had spurred them could no longer push their tired bodies into fresh effort. Then, clinging together, as if the touch of flesh against flesh was a defense against the insanity behind, they sat on the floor, dragging in the dead air in ragged, painful gasps.

TWELVE

"This—is—an—open—passage." Logan's warning came in separated words.

He was right. There was nothing to prevent that which had hunted Widders from prowling into this dark tunnel. Perhaps even now it lurked in the dim reaches ahead.

The arm Hosteen had flung about Logan's heaving shoulders tightened spasmodically. He must not let panic crowd out reason—that would deliver them both over to death. They had to keep thinking clearly.

"We have the grenades and the torch," he reassured himself as well as his companion. "Widders did not have his equipment—no light or weapon. It was a miracle he got even this far."

The shudders that had been shaking Logan were not so continuous.

"Scared as a paca rat caught in a grain bin!" The answer came with a ghost of the old wry humor Logan had always summoned to front disaster. "Never broke and ran like that before, though."

"That was enough to make both of us bolt," Hosteen replied. "You didn't see me holding back any, did you? But now I think we are past the trapped paca rat stage."

Logan's hand tightened on Hosteen's forearm in a grip of rough affection and then fell away. "You're right, brother. We've moved up a few steps in the panic scale—maybe now we're on the level of a frawn bull. But I want to be a tough yoris before we face somethin' alive and kickin'."

"Two yoris it is," Hosteen agreed. "I'd say keep straight ahead, but at less of a scamper."

He fingered the atom torch indecisively. If he switched that on, would the beam signal a lurker? But the advantage of light over dark won. With the enemy revealed in the light, they would have a chance to use their grenades.

As the passage continued to bore ahead through the stuff of the mountain, Hosteen marveled at the extent of the under-the-surface work. More than just the first mountain must be occupied by this labyrinth. He was sure they were well beyond the height up which the Norbies had originally driven their captives.

There were no signs that anything had come this way before them, and the first stark shock of Widders' end lost some of its impact on their minds. Hosteen sighted a gray glimmer ahead and switched off the torch so that they could approach another tunnel mouth warily.

Here projections hung down from overhead and stood up out of the floor of the passage, so they passed between two rows of pointed objects as thick as a man's leg. And set in a curved space well above their heads were three ovals of a blood-red, transparent substance through which light streamed in gory beams.

What lay beyond the opening was sun heat—the sun heat of the parched outer world, where the Big Dry reigned uncontrolled.

They hunched down between those pointed pillars, shielded their eyes against the punishing glare, and tried to pick out some route across that seared landscape.

In the shimmer of the heat waves there was a thin line of poles running—with a gap here and there—into the distance, just as the poles had marked the sonic barrier before the pens.

Hosteen used the lenses to trace that line, but the glare of that open oven was as deceptive as the foggy murk of the interior cavern.

"We'll have to lay up and wait for dark." Logan drew his knees up to his chest and folded his arms about them. "Nothin' could last for a half hour out there now."

How far did that guiding line of poles stretch? Could one find shelter at the end of that path before the coming of another day? And was this indeed open country?

"Open country?" Hosteen repeated questioningly.

"You think this might be another controlled cavern, to hold things enjoyin' bein' baked?"

"There are those poles—they must have run a sonic through here once." Hosteen pointed out the obvious.

"And there are a lot of gaps in that now, too." Logan squinted to study the way ahead. "Do we go back—or do we try it?"

"I'd say try it—at least part way. If night does come here, we can try and turn back if we can't see an end within safe travel distance."

"That makes sense," Logan conceded. "We wait."

Hope was thin. Much depended now on whether this was another cavern under weather control—the wrong kind of control for them—or the open. For human eyes, there was no looking up into the inferno that marked the possible sky. Hosteen had thought that the heat and glare when they first reached the end of the passage had been that of early afternoon. So they would wait for a night that might never fall or start the long trail back to that distant cave into which the Norbies had sealed them.

Uneasily they slept in turn, keeping watch as the time crept leadenly by. Suddenly, Hosteen was aroused from a doze by Logan's shaking.

"Look!"

Where the light had been—a yellow-white their eyes could meet only with actual pain—there was now a reddish glow. The Terran had seen its like too many times to be mistaken. Yes, there was a night out there, and it was now on its way. They need only wait for true dusk and then follow the road marked by the pole line.

They ate, drank sparingly of their water, and waited impatiently for the red to deepen to purple, the purple that meant freedom. But as they waited, Hosteen walked forward between the projections, his senses alert—to what? There was no sound out of the desert ahead, nothing moving there.

With the lenses he could follow the pole line well ahead—bare rock, the poles, with gaps in their marching line. No vegetation, no place for any living thing he had seen yet on Arzor. Yet, inside him, there was a growing fear of that sere landscape, a tension far higher in pitch

143

than any he had known before in any of the tunnels and caverns they had traversed.

"What is it?"

Startled, Hosteen looked back over his shoulder. Logan had been testing the fastening of the canteens. But now he, too, was staring with narrowed eyes into the open.

"I don't know," the other answered slowly. "This—is—strange—"

They had run in open horror and fear from the place where Widders lay. Now, as the Terran weighed one emotion against the other, he was sure that the sensation he was experiencing was not the same as they had known earlier. Where that, in part, had been physical fear, this was a more subtle thing, twitching at mind and not at body.

"We'll go—" Logan did not make a question of that, rather a promise that was half challenge to what lay ahead. His jaw was set, and the stubbornness that had made him go his own way so often in the past was in the ascendant now, setting him to face what he shrank from.

"We'll go," Hosteen assented. Every fiber of his body fought against his will in this. What had begun as an uneasiness was now a shivering, quivering revolt of one deeply rooted part of him against the iron form of his determination. Yet, he knew that he could not refuse to go out there and face whatever waited, for if he did, he would be broken in some strange, inexplicable way that would leave him as crippled as if he had been shorn of a leg or an arm.

Dusk—they moved forward, shoulder to shoulder, coming out of the tunnel mouth. Logan caught at Hosteen and dragged him half around.

For a wild second or two the Terran thought he was facing the source of his subtle fears. Then he guessed the truth. The tunnel mouth had been carved into a weird and horrible image. They had emerged from a fanged mouth, the open gullet of a three-eyed monster fashioned after the skull they had discovered on the shore of the underground lake. The eyes glinted—those were the oval red patches they had sighted from within. The wrinkled snout—Hosteen did not doubt for a moment that the artist who had designed that portal knew well a living model.

"Could that be the full size of three eyes?" Logan found his voice and attempted some of his old lightness of tone.

"Who knows—at least we came out instead of going in."

"And we may regret that yet!"

They trotted on, away from the mask doorway. Underfoot, the space bordered by the pole line was smooth, though Hosteen's torch did not show any trace of paving. Anyway, it provided good footing for the pace they must set, until midnight told them whether they could advance or must retreat into three eyes' waiting jaws.

Not a sound, not a stir of breeze. But—Hosteen stopped and swung the pencil beam of the torch off the path before him to a pool of shadow under a pinnacle of rock to the left. Light on rocks—just that, bare rocks. Yet, the moment before the ray had touched that surface, he had been certain something lurked there, slinking around that pile, sniffing its way toward the pole path. He could have sworn he heard the pattern of its gusty breathing, the faint scrape of talon on rock, the sound of a stone disturbed!

"Nothin' there!"

Logan, also? Had he heard, sensed, believed something had been out there?

"To the left!" Logan's hand was on his wrist now, bringing the torch beam about, to shine it directly into a crevice in the ground. Of course! The thing must be crouching there, just waiting for them to draw opposite and then—!

Bare rock—empty crevice, nothing!

"There—there has to be somethin'." Logan's words were marked with the determination to hold his emotions in check. "They had a sonic barrier for protection, didn't they?"

"Once they had it," replied Hosteen.

Ghosts—spirits? The ghosts of the builders of this road, the artist who had carved that dragon mask—or of the weird life that had lived on this sun-rusted plain from which the builders protected themselves in their journeyings?

He started on, Logan matching him step by step. They started slowly and then their speed built, as the need to get past all those rock outcrops, all those sinister crevices and dips, ate at their self-control.

Croaking—or was it husky breathing? There—! Hosteen was sure this time he had spotted the danger point, not too far ahead in a shadow pool by a hillock. He gripped a grenade in one hand, ready, brought the torch up with the quick flick of a stunner draw, aiming the light as he might the stupefying ray.

Rock—only rock.

"Steady!" Hosteen was not even aware he had given himself that command aloud.

If his imagination was at work, perhaps he could bend

it to his own purposes. Suppose there was some living thing out there playing games, able to project an impression of its presence where it was not in order to confuse enemies? Hosteen's training of the team had made him open-minded in matters dealing with mental relationships between men and animals—and, who knows, perhaps some of the same techniques could work between man and alien?

That faculty, which had tied him to Surra, Hing, and Baku, in part to the stallion Rain and other non-mutant-bred living creatures, could he use it to detect what was behind this nerve-breaking attack? Something assured him that this was an attack, far more subtle and devastating than any physical thrust out of the night.

Just as a blindfolded man might feel his way cautiously through unknown territory, so did Hosteen reach out to try to contact what lay waiting out there. Intelligence—was he dealing with intelligence, alien but still to be reckoned so by human standards? Or did he front some protective device set up to warn off intruders, just as the sonic barrier had been erected to protect the rulers of the pen cavern?

A touch of what—awareness? The Terran was sure he had met that, so sure that he paused and slowly pivoted toward the dark space from which that twinge of contact had seemed to come. Was it his imagination that supplied the rest? He could never have offered any proof, but from that instant Hosteen believed that he had had a momentary mental meeting with someone or something that had once lived in communication with the builders of this mountain maze, as he lived in concert with the team.

And he believed it so firmly that he strove to hold to

147

that thread, to impress upon that unknown creature his desire for a meeting, as he could in part impose his will on the team. Only, the frail and fleeting contact was snapped almost as quickly as it was made.

What flooded in to follow was the anger of an aroused guardian or an embattled survivor—an attack through mental and emotional gates so intense that, had it persisted, perhaps both men would have broken under it.

Shadows boiled, twisted, crawled, slunk in upon them. The light beam stabbed each menace into nothingness, only to have another take its place. Logan called out hoarsely, snatched up stones clawed loose handfuls of soil to hurl them at that invisible menace now ringing them in. And it built up and up!

There was rage in this—as if behind some unclimbable barrier the three-eyed monster of the caverns raced back and forth, eager to get at them. And it was when that impression grew on Hosteen that he gasped out an order:

"Stand still!"

Logan froze, his arm half up to throw a rock.

"We go on—"

Hosteen obeyed his own order, his legs moving stiffly, his active mind arguing against such folly. There—there *was* something crawling across the path just ahead—waiting—ready— To the left—two—converging on the strip through which the men must pass within moments. They were surrounded.

Logan shuffled along. Sweep, sweep—the torch opened the secrets of shadows. But the pressure against the intruders was reaching the point past which Hosteen was afraid he could not hold.

With a snarl Logan faced left, his hand went to his

belt, and he lobbed one of the grenades into the dark. The resulting burst of light left them blinded for a second or two.

Then—nothing! As there had been the explosion, so now there was an answering burst of energy in their minds. Then, only empty land under the night sky—a landscape now without any life in it.

Shaken, they stood breathing hard with rib-stretching gasps and then began to run. Again their road approached the foot of a mountain, and they could reach that before the sun rose.

Underfoot, the trail was rising slowly but steadily above the surface of the ground. When Hosteen turned the light on that road, they saw that now it was fashioned of the black substance used elsewhere to coat tunnel walls.

They were well above the general level of the valley when the road ended in a wide wedge of black, the narrow end of which touched against a solid cliff wall in which there was no discernible break. To all their inspection with hand and torch, there was no door there, no way ahead. This was the end of the trail they had been following for so long.

"A landin' mat for 'copters, d' you suppose?" Logan asked after they had made a second circling exploration of the wedge. He was sitting cross-legged on the smooth black surface, his hands resting on his knees. "What now—do we start back?"

Privately the Terran doubted if they could now make that return trip before the day broke. Though they had not come so far in actual distance, their struggle with the shadows had been exhausting. He knew that fatigue of both mind and body rode him, made him flinch at the

149

thought of back-tracking. Yet if they wanted to live, they must do that before sunrise.

He had hunkered down on the pavement and was flashing his torch back forth across its surface for no conscious reason. Then his eyes sighted the pattern there, and his dull mind became alert. There was a circular strip of glassy, glossy black, which began at the point where the road met the wedge and then spiraled around and around until it ended in a circle just large enough for a man to stand upon.

Why he went into action then he could never afterwards explain. It was all a part of the weird influence of this place. He only knew that this he must do at once.

Crossing to the beginning of that spiral, he began to walk along the route it marked, around and around, approaching the center point and concentrating upon keeping his boots firmly planted on the slick surface, in no way touching the duller borders.

Dimly he was aware of Logan asking questions, demanding answers. But that sound, the words, meant nothing now. The most important thing in the world was to walk that path without deviation or error. The circle in the center could not be rightly entered in any other way, and it was a door.

Door? demanded another part of his brain. How? Why?

Hosteen fought down all questions. To walk the spiral slowly, cautiously, with all his powers of concentration, with no careless boot-toe touch beyond its border, he had to fit one foot almost directly before the other, balance like a man walking the narrowest of mountain ledges.

This way only was it safe. Safe? He dismissed that query also.

Hosteen was in the circle now, turning to face the way they had come, toward those other dark mountains under which must lie the cavern of the pens, all the rest of the holdings of the forgotten alien invaders. Then he stood waiting. For what? clamored common sense.

Dark—and the sensation of being totally free from the boundaries set by time and space and everything mankind used to measure distance in two dimensions.

Then light and another path to be walked, another spiral, this glowing—not to be taken by one booted foot set carefully ahead of the other but mentally. And with the same concentration he had given to his action on the wedge, so did he now do this. He was at its center, with another kind of light rising in a haze all about him.

THIRTEEN

The process was like waking from a deep sleep. Hosteen fought a groggy disorientation, became aware of where he was and that he no longer stood in the open on a wedge under a starred sky. Instead, his boots were planted on a block of glassy material, and around him was another kind of light, a rusty glow that had no visible source unless it was born out of the air.

"Logan!" He demanded an answer, yet knew that none would come. In this place he was alone, alone with the knowledge that his species was not of this place—or time—that he was in strange exile.

The training the Terran had had acted against panic. He had followed an alien road but one that had had purpose—and it had brought him here. Now he must discover where "here" was.

Leaping from the block, Hosteen looked about. He was in a very small room—a room of three walls meeting in sharply angled corners. And those walls were unbroken by any openings of windows or doors. Again panic threatened as he faced the possibility of being imprisoned in this box. There was no spiral path to lead him out, only the block, the three walls, the ceiling over his head, the floor under him. And to his sight, walls, floor and ceiling were solid.

But eyes were not the only sense organs he possessed. Hosteen approached the nearest wall and ran his finger tips along its slick surface. It was glassy smooth to the touch and a little warm—where he had expected the chill of stone.

He walked the full length of that wall until his fingers pointed into the sharp angle of the corner. Then Hosteen turned along the second. He had reached the mid-point of that when there was a change in the surface not perceptible to the eye. Three depressions appeared, not quite the size or shape of his fingers, since he pushed in with room to spare. But he was reminded of the finger locks used on inner-system planets, locks that would open only to print patterns of their owners' flesh ridges. If this was such a lock, he had no hope, for the fingers—or appendages—which had set it had long since vanished from Arzor. But the Terran pressed his fingers into those hollow desperately, hoping for but not really expecting action.

A tingling in each of those three fingers, spreading up across the back of his hand, reaching his wrist, now into his forearm. A tingling—or was it a sucking—a pull of strength out of his tendons and muscles to be absorbed into those glassy pits of the wall? Hosteen supported his wrist now with his other hand because, when he tried to withdraw his fingers, he found them gripped in a suction beyond his power to break.

He leaned against the wall, twisting his right wrist with

153

the aid of his other hand, striving to break that contact, feeling strength seep out of him as clearly as if he could watch the draining process in action along every vein, through every finger-tip pore.

Then the wall shivered, shimmered, to break from ceiling to floor. A strip of surface three feet wide where his hand had touched vanished, and he fell through, then crawled out of the triangular box to lie on the floor of another, much larger space. At least he was out of the cage!

Logan! Logan left back there on the plain to await the sun—and the burning death of the Big Dry. Logan! Would he—*could* he—take the same escape road Hosteen had found?

The Terran wavered to his feet, nursing his right hand and arm against his chest. The skin was pallid, the hand itself numb, and his utmost efforts to move the fingers resulted only in a slight twitching. Heavy and cold, he thrust it inside his shirt against his bare chest. But for a moment he forgot that as he looked around him.

The dusky, reddish light of the box was lightened here into the golden radiance he had remembered from the Cavern of the Hundred Gardens. With the hope of another such find, Hosteen stumbled forward to a waist-high barrier just a few feet ahead. Then he was looking down from a galley into, not the gardens of his hopes, but into a vast assembly of machines and installations. And from it rose a subdued hum, a vibration of air. These installations were not only in working order, they were working!

Yet, nowhere down those rows could he see any tenders, no human or robot inspectors as one might find in off-world machine plants.

"Started—then left to run—forever?" he whispered.

For what purpose?

He started along the gallery, hunting a way down to that center hall. The room was a vast oval, and his entrance had been at one end. Now as he skirted that waist-high barrier, watching the space below, Hosteen continued to marvel at the size and complexity of the installations.

The Terran's own training had been in psycho-biology. An Amerindian had an ancient tie with nature and the forces of nature, which was his strength, just as other races had come to rely more and more on machines. It was upon such framework that his whole education had been based, his sympathies centered. So, both inborn and special conditioning had made of him a man aloof from, and suspicious of, machines. One had to be anti-tech to be a Beast Master.

Now his disinterest in machines was growing to a repulsion as he looked down into the well of the vast chamber. The minds that had conceived and produced the Gardens he could understand. He might, though he did not find any kinship with them, grasp the motives of the pen keepers—they had dealt with living things. But these installations put a wall between him and those who had once been active here.

His growing dislike was not blunting his powers of observation. Hosteen believed that only a small number of the machines below were in use. He passed by whole sections where there were none of those subtle waves of power rising or falling. Then he saw the platform.

He was raised not more than a Terran foot or so above the floor of the main hall, and it was backed by a tall boarding, reaching almost to the balcony on which he stood. There were lines in relief on that boarding, running in intricate tangles. One made an irregular circle, and it glowed—glowed with a pulsating light of the same mauve that made fair Arzor sky different from Terra's lost blue.

Two other lines also showed color. One, a golden yellow, began in a straight column near the foot of the board and ran up to a mid-point, where, though there was a many-branched channel of the same tubing above, it stopped. And this pulsated with a faster beat. The third—Hosteen caught sight of the third, his attention riveted on it, startled.

That was a spiral leading to a dot. And as he watched, the light grew brighter, until its brilliance was more than his eyes could bear. The light traveled along that spiral, approached the dot, flashed there for an eye-searing second or two.

Then, the whole pattern of spiral and dot was lifeless, dead as the hundred other designs of tubing on that board. But he had not been mistaken. The light had been there—had been so bright he could not watch it, any more than a man could watch the sun of the Big Dry.

Hosteen turned and began to run back toward the triangular box from which he had emerged.

Logan—that shining swirl on the board could mean that Logan had taken the spiral and circle path out of the valley! He could be coming here!

The Terran's wild pace was such that he brought up against the now solid wall of the cubby almost as he had crashed against the inner wall of the cave where the Norbies had sealed them in to begin this adventure.

"Logan!" he shouted and heard the sound deadened, swallowed up in the reaches of the hall. Hosteen pounded on the wall with his good hand, drew the still numb right fist out of his shirt and tried to feel for any hollows on this side of the wall.

Pits for fingers. He had found them—this time with the digits of his left hand. He hesitated to deaden that too, as the right now was—to render himself helpless. But to get Logan out—free from the desert trap. Hosteen pushed his left hand against the smooth surface, fitted three finger tips into the waiting depressions, and waited, not without an inward shrinking, for the tingling—the sucking.

This time the response came more quickly, as might a lock long unused respond more rapidly to the second turning of a key. The panel faded, was gone— He looked into the cubby to see bare walls, empty space—nothing else.

Hosteen had been so sure he would again face Logan that for a moment he could not accept that emptiness.

"Logan!" Again the cry, which had come with the full force of his lung power, was muted, flattened into an echoing murmur of sound.

Already the gap in the wall was forming into its old solidity. He had been so sure. Hosteen lifted his numbed right hand uncertainly to his head. His distrust of the machines, of the power he did not understand, was a hot fire in him, a heat that reached into his cold, blanched fingers. He crooked them with a supreme effort, felt nails scrape the skin of his forehead.

The spiral on the board—it *had* been a miniature of the design in the valley, the pathway that had deposited him in this place. And he was certain that when the tube had glowed, it had signaled the use of that path, or another like it. So—perhaps that board held the secret!

Hosteen lurched away from the now solid wall and started along the other arm of the balcony, searching for a way down to the platform. In the end, he found the exit, an unobtrusive opening back against the hall wall, giving on a series of notched steps. He held the guard rail of that steep stair, noting with a fierce joy that the lack of feeling in his hand was ebbing—though to raise it was still like trying to raise a leaden weight attached to his wrist.

Now he was on ground level, picking a way among the machines to the platform. The majority of the installations were encased in block coverings, and these towered well above Hosteen's head as he hurried down the aisle.

There was no dust here as there had been in some of the tunnels, no sign that this chamber had been in existence for eons, perhaps abandoned for centuries. Yet, he was sure all of this was a part of the vanished Sealed Cave civilization.

Hosteen had almost reached the platform when he paused, took cover. A hum came from ahead, rising from a low note, hardly to be distinguished from the general voice of the machines, to a sound more impressive than his own shouts on the balcony—as if this sound was normal here, the voice of man not.

On the tube encrusted board another design had glowed into life. First blue—then white, bright enough to make him cover his eyes. When he looked again, there was a man on the platform, facing the board!

"Logan!" His lips shaped the name, but luckily he did not call aloud, for that was not Logan.

The stranger was taller than Hosteen's half-brother, and he was not wearing Norbie dress. In fact, those green coveralls were familiar. That was the Service Center uniform Hosteen himself had worn for over a year at the Rehab station, where the homeless forces of Terrans had been held until they could either be assigned to new worlds or put through pyscho-conditioning.

Slowly the Terran edged around the boxed installation. The LB had been transporting Rehab men when it had crashed out on the mountain. Could this be a survivor, driven into the maze as Logan and he had been? Yet, the actions of the man on the platform were not those of a lost and bewildered castaway; they were the assured motions of a tech on duty.

His head turned from side to side as if he studied the twists and turns of that web of tubing. Then he moved half face to Hosteen.

Unmistakable human features, but painted over with the patterns of a Norbie Drummer—red circles about the eyes, a complicated series of lines on each cheek—just as Hosteen had seen on the faces of the warriors of the Blue. And slung about the other's neck was a small "medicine" tambour. An off-worlder who united in his person the make-up of a primitive medicine man and the actions of one understanding and tending the complex controls of a vanished civilization!

The stranger stretched out both hands and moved them across a line of small bulbs in a carefully governed sweep. To Hosteen's watching, he did not actually touch any, merely passed the flat of a palm over them.

And the board answered. That line of yellow light bubbling in the vertical shaft broke through whatever barrier had controlled it and threaded up and out through a dozen, two dozen filaments, each branching and rebranching until the lighted whole was the skeleton of a leafless tree. The soaring light reached the very top of the board. And around him Hosteen was conscious of an ingathering of energy, a poising of power to be launched.

Far away, but still awesomely loud, there was a clap of thunder, pounding on in a series of receding rolls. Hosteen cowered against the machine.

He closed his eyes for a second and felt as if he stood in the center of a storm's full fury. He could sense, if he could not see, the savage lash of lightning across a night-black sky under clouds as heavy as the rocks over which they clustered. And, small, weak man-thing that he was, he was, he could only seek shelter from elements to which man was nothing.

Yet, when he opened his eyes again, there was only a man in a faded coverall watching a light pulse through a transparent tube. The stranger's hand swept again over the bulbs. And the tree began to die, the yellow shrinking, retreating along the filaments, leaving the tubes empty. Once more it was only in the trunk from which the branches arose.

The storm ended. But the stranger was still intent upon the board. He paced along it, sometimes pausing for long moments, inspecting this and that pattern of webbing. Once or twice he put out a finger to trace some loop of tube. And Hosteen thought that perhaps he was unfamiliar with the function of that particular hookup.

At last he came to the end of the platform nearest the Terran and stepped up upon a small dais. To his right now was another line of bulbs. Holding his hands a foot apart before those, the man brought palm against palm in sharp clap, as if applauding some triumph. Then—

Hosteen stepped away from the shadow of the machine that had sheltered him. The dais was empty, just as empty as if the man was as immaterial as that which had hunted them in the dry valley.

The Terran could accept his journey via the spiral path. But this was something else, more akin to the old magic that his grandfather had talked of before Terra became a roasted cinder.

He made himself mount the platform, go to the dais. There was no break in the flooring, no possible exit for a solid human body. Just as he had recoiled in spirit from the machines in the hall, so was he now repulsed by this device. Yet, as he had been impelled to follow the spiral path in the valley, so now his hands moved against his will. He copied the gesture the stranger had used, palm met palm in a half-hearted clap.

Again the terrible giddiness of being nowhere on earth, or in any dimension known to his species, held him. But a spark of triumph battled fear—again he had used one of the tricks of this place boldly.

Hosteen opened his eyes. Ahead was daylight—not the artificial light of a cavern but true and honest sunlight. He was in a mountain tunnel heading to the outer world.

A murmur of sound ahead, and Hosteen dropped to his hands and knees, making the rest of that journey with all the caution of his Commando training. Daylight—the hour was well into morning he believed. Yet, there was no glare as there had been in the valley of the wedge or that was common in the country outside the wall of the Blue.

Had the devices of the Sealed Cave people put some film of protection between this taboo world and the blistering Dry sun? Had the same knowledge that had bored the tunnels and the caverns also brought weather control to the open? But this was no time for speculations.

Hosteen lay belly-flat at the tunnel mouth, then chose a crab-like crawl to take him out into the open and behind one of the abutments guarding the doorway.

Norbies were drawn up downslope, not in serried rows but in small groupings, each fronted by a flagged truce pole, headed by a Chief and a Drummer. Such a meeting of clans and tribes would amaze any settler. There were Norbies standing clan next to clan down there between whom there had been ceremonial blood feuds from long before the first Survey scout ship had discovered Arzor for Confederation star maps. Only a very big medicine could bring about such a truce against all ancient custom.

Shosonna, Nitra, Warpt, Ranag from the south—even Gousakla, and they were a coastal people who must have crossed a thousand miles at the worst season of the year to appear here. There were other totems of both clan and tribe Hosteen had never seen or heard described.

Counting, Hosteen made that tally of different poles more than a hundred, and he knew he could not see them all without emerging from his hiding place. By rude reckoning, every tribe on this continent must be represented!

The Drummers were busy, the beat of their individual tambours blending into a rhythm that stirred the blood. Lean yellow bodies swayed back and forth, answering that call, though not a booted foot stirred. Hosteen could smell the fug of burned vegetation, could sight trails of smoke. Only recently the whips of lightning had again been laid about the shoulders of the mountain.

Thud—thud—a crescendo of sound. Then, after a final crash, silence. Into that silence fell a delicate counter-tapping—as rain might come in a more gentle fashion after the growl of thunder.

Into the open some distance below came the man from the hall of machines. His fingers played on the taut head of his own drum, making that thin trickle of sound. And his tapping was picked up by first one and then another of the medicine men in that company.

FOURTEEN

The off-worlder threw both hands high above his head, a head that under the sun shown as brightly red-gold as the fires of the lightning.

He began to speak, and he did not use the hand signs of the settlers. The twittering bird notes—which authorities had sworn could not be shaped by human vocal cords or lips—poured from him. He was talking to the Norbies in their own tongue!

Shrill cries broke his first pause. Truce poles were tossed in the air until the fluttering of their totem streamers whirled in a crazy dance of ribbon strips.

Hosteen's mouth straightened into a hard line; his face was graven, without expresison, save that his eyes were watchful, as watchful as those of a man facing a death peril.

The signs were the same from world to world, race to race, species to species. This orator had the Norbies in the grip of a spell woven by his words. And he was inciting them to action! Their "big medicine" was working—alive! The trouble Quade and Kelson had smelled in the plains now walked openly in the Blue. Walked? No rather spoke with drum and voice—to urge what?

Hosteen's own inability to understand more than the emotions being aroused was a torment. But his doubts were resolved. Magic, if you wanted to call it that—but something his own inheritance recognized—was drugging their minds to provide a free path for unreasoning action, which could be used by that man in the off-world uniform with a Norbie painted face.

"Ani'iihii—" Hosteen spat.

Sorcerer was the right name for this witch man shaping disaster and death out of the words, as the witches of Terra long ago had shaped a man's death from a lock of his hair ceremoniously buried in a grave.

The drums replied with a beat that awoke a response in Hosteen's own hurrying blood. Just so, generations ago, halfway across the galaxy, had men of his own race drummed and danced before raiding. This was preparation for war.

And with such a collection of tribes, there could be only one answer to the identity of the intended enemy—the scattered holdings of the plains settlers, strung out thinly with leagues of open range land between each Center House, ripe for plucking by strike-and-run fighters. Norbies were warriors by tradition and training. It would take very little to turn them into an efficient guerrilla force that could wipe off-worlders from Arzor before they were aware of their danger.

The very nature of the country would fight for the natives at this season. Their carefully kept water secrets would make them far more mobile than any Patrol expeditionary force the settlers could call in.

Hosteen rubbed his forearm across his face. Nightmares out of the past provided spectres to follow a man for years. He had served on the fringe of a war that had involved not only worlds but solar systems, had seen the blotting out of nations and planets. Yes, the Patrol could be called in to end such a hit-and-run war—but afterwards, Arzor, as they knew it now, would cease to exist.

There was a final boom of drum—the orator was returning to the ledge of the tunnel, the Norbies ebbing back into the valley. Back to their village—to arm, to plan? Why? Hosteen could not pick the answer to that out of their twittering.

He worked a grenade out of his belt pouch. The stranger was on the ledge. Hosteen waited for a challenge, for some attack. But the other was staring straight before him, his eyes wide. He walked with a stiff, rocking pace. If he had locked the Norbies in some spell of eloquence, he was as tightly enchanted himself. Glancing neither to right nor left, he entered the passage.

This was the mountain on which the LB had landed. Hosteen watched the Norbies withdraw, tried to think. The LB—and Widders' story of those weak signals picked up by line camp coms. Just suppose the craft's com could still broadcast! A message might be sent to alert the plains!

The stranger could be hunted later—but to get to the LB now was worth the risk.

Surra—Baku—Gorgol. None of them had been brought to the village while Logan and he had been there. Were the three still at large?

Hosteen sent out once more that unvoiced, unheard rallying call of the team—tried to locate some mental radiation from bird or cat to reinstate once again their tight compact, so that man, cat, and eagle would not be three alone and adrift but a weapon, a defense such as Arzor, with all its hidden secrets, did not know.

"Baku!" He sent thought spinning like a lasso into the sky, striving to reach the mind behind those falcon-sharp eyes. But there was no answer.

"Surra!" Now he deserted the upper spaces and withdrew to the ground in search of one walking velvet-footed. "Surra!"

The answer he had ceased to hope for came like a stab of fire.

"Where?" His lips shaped the word as the query flew back along that tenuous thread of thought connection.

Impression of dark—of rock-walled passages. The cat must be somewhere within the mountain. Yes, Surra was there. And she lay in wait for some living thing now moving toward her. The orator?

The frustration that had rasped Hosteen moments earlier vanished. He worked the numbed line of mental contact just as he had the fingers of his numbed hand. Surra was an important part of him; without her, the composite entity that was the team was crippled, helpless as a man shorn of some important sense organ.

And he knew from the quality of her response, fierce, demanding, that that that lack had been hers also.

"The one coming"—he sent his message—"trail but do not take. Keep in touch with me."

Surra would take the stranger under surveillance. Hosteen was free to reach the LB. He swung down from the ledge and worked his way along the slope, using every bit of cover and scoutcraft he knew.

Drums again, faint—they must be in the village. He used a springy bush to lower himself into the clearing, where the sweet-sick scent of decay hung heavy. The offerings were still heaped about the rounded sides of the craft; the escape port on the top was closed.

Had it ever been opened or was the LB still sealed with a passenger list of dead men? The presence of the stranger argued that at least one of the castaways had escaped.

Hosteen climbed a sapling, which bent under his weight, allowing him to land near the tail. Slamming his hand down on the pressure lock of the hatch, he waited tensely.

With a squeak of protest, the port began to lift slowly. Hosteen's one fear vanished as he seized the edge of the door and forced it straight up. The LB had opened after its landing on Arzor; he was not about to enter a tomb.

The interior space of such a craft was limited, and from abandon-ship drill in the Service he knew its layout. Pushing between two rows of acceleration bunks set against each wall, he reached the nose, where the auto and hand pilots and the com set were to be found.

Side lights had gone on when he opened the hatch, showing him the wiring was still in order. Hosteen hunched into the small space before the com. He flicked the switch to open and was rewarded with a promising click-click of an expanding broadcast aerial, the purr of a working com. With finger on button, he tapped out the message he had composed on the way downhill.

The landing signals of this ship had registered months ago on the pickups of two line camps. Only because those camps were rarely visited had the signals gone undetected so long. And now both Quade and Kelson would have ment was open and empty. Save for the plasta foam pads He tapped out his warning twice by hand, setting it so on a repeat wire. Now that would go on broadcasting at ten revolutions an hour until it was turned off, and he intended to see that was impossible unless the com or the ship was destroyed.

Hosteen made adjustments, resealed the shield panel, and then went to explore the rest of the craft in the faint hope of discovering a weapon. But the stores' compartment was open and empty. Save for the plasta foam pads on the bunks, there was nothing left.

He was standing directly under the escape hatch, preparing to leave, when a roll of thunder startled him. Only reflex action saved his life as he slammed his hand on the seal button of the port.

Thunder again, but now muted into a distant mutter by the protection of the hull. The LB trembled under a blow. Hosteen scrambled for the pilot's seat, thumbed on the visa-screen—to view a roaring holocaust. If the fire that had lashed the mountan before had spared the LB, it did so no longer. The craft shook and reeled under streams of flame.

Would the insulation intended for the protection of space flight hold against this fierce concentration of energy? The force of that attack was twisting the ship around, might push it on down the slope.

Had the broadcast from the com alerted the stranger in the mountain, the message been picked up by some device of that other civilization? Hosteen was sure that this attack came from the Sealed Cave armory.

Surra! Hosteen braced himself in the shuddering cabin

as he strove to reach the cat. But once more he met only the solid barrier he had found that night when he had been prisoner in the Norbie village. Perhaps the fire cut off contact. A reasonable explanation if not a comforting one.

The LB was no longer on an even keel. Hosteen caught one of the stanchions supporting the nearest bunk. The visa-screen told him the whole craft was encased in wildly ranging flame. He was trapped with no defense but the walls of the ship.

He stretched out on a bunk and snapped the acceleration webbing to hold his body in place. If that bath of energy did roll the LB over a cliff, he could have that small protection.

The nose of the craft tilted down and the whole hull quivered as the dive picked up speed. Then there was a bone-wrenching crash as the ship met some obstruction head on. The visa-screen went blank. And the com—he thought that the com had not survived either. How many broadcasts had it made before the end? Enough for one full message to reach beyond the Peaks?

Hosteen lay sweating on the bunk, the LB now more vertical than horizontal. The cabin lights flickered, dimmed, then brightened again in a crazy dance of light and dark. Though the LB no longer moved, would a shifting of his own weight send it into another slide?

Freeing himself from the webbing, the Terran gingerly swung his feet to the floor, keeping a grip on the stanchion. The steeply sloping deck did not move as he clawed his way to the pilot compartment to discover chaos behind a buckled wall. The com was dead. Well, if this attack had been to silence the warning, the enemy had won the first skirmish. That didn't mean he would also win the war.

Without the visa-screen. Hosteen was blind. Did the fire still bathe the ship? He wedged into one of the tilted bunks again, rested his forehead on his crooked arm, and bent all the energy left in his mind and body into a concentration aimed at Surra.

"Here—" The word she could not form aloud was a whisper in his brain.

"The man?"

"Here—" A repetition of her first answer or an assurance that she still had her quarry under observation?

"In the mountain?"

"So—"

"Then stay—follow—" he ordered.

Maybe his ability to reach the dune cat meant that the fire no longer ringed the LB. But to get to the hatch now required some acrobatic maneuvering. And when his first attempt to open the port did not succeed, Hosteen knew the starkness of dread. Had the flames sealed his escape hole?

Then, though with protest, the hatch moved as he beat on it with one frantic fist, holding to his support with the other. Smoke swirled in a choking blue fog, burning his eyes, strangling him with coughing until the air filter of the cabin thinned it.

Smoke, heat, but no sign of active flames. Hosteen retreated to rip and pry at the plasta foam covering of the bunks, removing the stuff in tattered strips. Half of these he draped over the rim of the hatch opening, pushing the material through to lie across the heated shell of the LB. The rest he took with him as he climbed out on the temporarily protected area.

The side of the LB bore the lick marks of fire, and around it the ground was charred black. Upslope, small blazes still crackled in bushes.

Hosteen worked fast, tying lengths of the plasta foam about his feet and legs above knee level. The tough synthetic fabric would be a shield against the heat. With more scraps mittening his hands and covering his arms, he crawled up the tail of the LB, leaped for the top of a fire-blackened rock, and started the climb back to the tunnel ledge.

Back in the mountain Surra would be his eyes, a part of himself projected. He could track the stranger, perhaps find Logan. Logan!

All he could do to warn the plains had been done. The holdings would have to take their chances while he faced the heart of the trouble here and now.

Tap—tap—tap—

The Terran was an animal, startled, snarling in defiance, his teeth showing white between tightened lips as Surra's could upon occasion. He stood still, watching that figure come out of a copse that had escaped the lick of the fire.

A cloak spread like huge wings of a mantling bird—a Drummer! And there was no knife in Hosteen's belt, no stunner. He had only his two hands—

However, the other had no more. By tradition, the Norbie would be unarmed—depending upon his power for his protection. And no native would raise hand against a Drummer, even one of an enemy tribe. The vengeance taken by "medicine" was swift, sure, and frightful.

But if this one depended upon that custom now, he would have a rude, perhaps fatal awakening. Hosteen had to get his hands on the tambour the native carried, silence it before the Drummer could use it to arouse the warriors.

The Terran tensed for another leap. His body arched up; his bandaged hands caught up burned and fire-scorched wood. He moved with the sure speed of a trained fighting man.

Tap—tap—

There had been no acceleration in that soft patter, no deepening of the beat. No settler understood drum talk, but Hosteen wondered. He had expected an outburst of alarm when he was sighted. What he heard as he charged was a calm sequence of small sounds—like a friendly greeting. Instead of throwing his body forward in a tackle, he halted to face the enemy squarely.

"Ukurti!"

Fingers lifted from the tight drumhead—moved in talk.

"Where do you go?"

Sharp, to the point. Hosteen tugged at the wrappings on his hands, freed his fingers to reply:

"To the mountain."

He dared not risk evasion, not with this Drummer whom he knew to be not the witch doctor of scoffing off-worlders but a real power.

"You have been to the mountain once."

"I have been once," Hosteen assented. "I go again—for in this mountain walks evil."

"That is so." The quick agreement surprised Hosteen.

"He who drums for the Zamle totem says that?"

"One who drums, drums true, or else the power departs from him. In the mountain is one who says that thunder answers his drum, that he brings lightning to his service."

"It has been heard, so has it been seen." Again Hosteen kept to the strict truth.

"Fire has answered; that is truth. And because of this warriors bind arrowheads to war shaft, chant songs of trophies to be smoked in the Thunder Houses."

"Yet this is not good."

"It is not good!" Ukurti's head pushed forward; his paint-ringed eyes on either side of his boldly arched nose were those of Baku sighting prey before she was quite poised for the killing swoop. "This one who wears the name of Ukurti has been to the place of sky ships' landing and has seen the powers of those who ride from star to star. They, too, drum thunder and raise lightning of a kind—but it is not born of the true power of Arzor." His booted foot stamped the black ground, and a tiny puff of ash arose.

"Before them, others walked the same trails—even here on Arzor. To the strangers their power, to us ours. This is an old trail, newly opened once again. And in it lie many traps for the heedless and those who want to believe because it serves their false dreams. I who bear the name of Ukurti in this life and who have the right to speak of this power and that"—again he stroked the drumhead gently, bringing a muted purr of sound from its surface—"say that no good comes of a trail that leads to blood running free on the ground, the blood of those who have shared water, hunted, eaten meat with us, and welcomed in their tents my people."

"And he-who-drums-thunder here says that this shedding of blood is right—that the war arrow is to be put to the string against my people?"

"That is so."

174

"For what purpose does he demand a shedding of blood?"

"That his power may eat and grow strong, giving many gifts to those who serve it."

"But his power is not the power you follow."

"That is so. And this is an evil thing. Now I say to you, who also have a power that is from beyond the stars and lies within you, go up to this man who is of your own kind and set your power against him."

"And you will not drum up those to hunt me?"

"Not so. Between us is a peace pole. It has been set upon me to—in a small way—smooth your trail."

"You knew I was here—you were waiting for me?"

"I knew. But no man explains the working of his own medicine. This is a thing of my power."

"Pardon, Drummer. I do not ask the forbidden." Hosteen's fingers made swift and contrite apology.

"But from here you walk alone," Ukurti continued.

"Do all the clans walk the trail leading to the running of blood?" Hosteen ventured.

"Not all—yet," but the Drummer did not enlarge upon that.

"And this I must do alone?"

"Alone."

"Then, Drummer, give me of your luck wish before I depart." Hosteen signed the formal request made by all Norbie warriors leaving a clan camp. He waited. Did the other's favor reach to actually invoking his power for an off-world alien or did his aid only consist of standing aside to let Hosteen fight his own battle? The difference could mean a great deal to the waiting Terran.

FIFTEEN

A breeze swirled ash, cooled earth, drove away the smoke and stench of fire, and pulled at the edge of the Drummer's feather cloak. Ukurti stared down at the tambour, which he held in both hands, as if he were reading on the tightly stretched skin of its head some message. His fingers tapped out a small burst of sharp notes while he spoke. Though that twittering was unintelligible to Hosteen, he thought he detected in it a rhythm that could be either a blessing or a curse. Then Ukurti's hands left the drum and made signs the Terran could understand.

"Go in power, one who knows the song of the wind, the whisper of growing things, the minds of beasts and birds. Go in power; do what must be done. In this moment the war arrow is balanced upon a finger. So light a thing as this wind may wreck a world."

It was more than Hosteen had dared hope the Drummer would ever grant him—not the blessing and good will for a warrior departing into danger but the outright promise of one wizard to another who also dealt in things unseen, a promise of power to be added to power.

In return, he accorded Ukurti the salute of upraised palms, which was the greeting of equal to equal, before he turned and started for the waiting tunnel mouth.

But in his hurry the Terran was also cautious. Ukurti had said nothing of any other natives being on the mountain, but that was no reason to disregard the possibility of more Drummers or warriors being drawn to the fire about the LB.

Hosteen reached the ledge of the tunnel without being sighted or trailed. And there he met Surra's warning. The stranger was returning in haste to the outer world. Coming to see the result of the fire attack?

The Terran had the grenades. But a dead enemy could not talk and might well provide a martyr whose influence after death could unleash destruction across the plains. A prisoner, not a dead man, was what Hosteen desired. With Surra's aid he could have that future captive already boxed. Only—

This was like running against an invisible wall. There was no pain such as the sonic barrier had spun around those who strove to pass it. No pain—only immobility, a freezing of every muscle against which Hosteen fought vainly. As helpless as he had been in the net of the Norbies, so was he again, held so for the coming of the enemy.

Helpless as to body, yes, but not in mind. Hosteen gave Surra an order. How far away was that chase—the man running to inspect his catch, the cat, unseen, unsensed by her quarry, padding at an ever quickening trot behind?

Just as Hosteen could plan, he could also hear. Ukurti

had not been alone on the mountain. The whistle of more than one. Norbie reached him, unmuffled by the morning wind. He did not credit the Shosonna medicine man with any treachery—such a promise as the other had given him when they parted would damn the Drummer who made it in false faith. No, his being held for the kill was not Ukurti's doing.

Surra—and Baku. He must try again to reach the eagle. Cat and bird might be his only defensive weapons. The cat he made contact with—the bird, no answer. And now the stranger broke from the tunnel mouth.

Taller than the Terran, his skin whitely fair under the paint of the natives, his hair ruddy bright, he stood there breathing hard. With both hands, he held at breast level a sphere that Hosteen eyed apprehensively. It was too like the antiperso grenades.

Then it was the other's eyes, rather than his hands and their burden, that drew the Beast Master's attention. Back at the Rehab Separation Center more than a year ago, he had seen that look in many eyes, too many eyes. Terran units brought in from active Service at the close of the war to discover their world gone—families, homes, everything lost—had had men in their ranks with such eyes. Men had gone mad and turned their weapons on base personnel, on each other, on themselves. And taking a cue from that past, Hosteen schooled his voice to the bark of an official demand.

"Name, rank, serial number, planet!"

There was a stir far down in the set glare of those eyes. The other's lips moved soundlessly, and then he spoke aloud.

"Farver Dean, Tech third rank, Eu 790, Cosmos" he replied in Galactic basic.

A tech of the third rank, 700 in his Service—not only a trained scientist but one of genius level! No wonder this man had been able to understand and use some of the secrets of the Cavern people.

Dean advanced another step or two, studying Hosteen. The face paint disguised much of his expression, but his attitude was one of puzzlement.

"Who are you?" he asked in return.

"Hosteen Storm, Beast Master, AM 25, Terra." Hosteen used the same old formula for reply.

"Beast Master," the other repeated. "Oh, of the Psych-Anth boys?"

"Yes."

"Nothing here for you, you know." Dean shook his head slowly from side to side. "This is a tech matter, not one for the nature boys."

Nature boys—the old scoffing term that underlined the split between the two branches of special Service. If Dean already had such hostility to build upon and was mentally unbalanced— Hosteen put away that small fear. At least the tech was talking, and that slowed any drastic action.

"We had no orders about you either." he stated. If Dean thought this was a service affair, so much the better. And how did the tech hold him prisoner? Was the device controlling the stass field in that sphere the other nursed so close to his chest? If that were so, Hosteen had a better chance than if his invisible bonds were manipulated by some machine back in the mountain.

Dean shrugged. "Doesn't concern me. You'll have to blast off—this is a tech affair."

His attitude was casual, far too casual. Hosteen smelled and tasted danger as he had a few times before in his life:

"Can't very well blast off while you have me in stass, can I?"

The other smiled, the stretch of facial muscles pulling the pattern lines on his cheeks into grotesque squares and angles.

"Stass—the nature boys can't fight stass!" His laugh was almost a giggle. Then he was entirely sober. "You thought you could trick me," he said dispassionately. "I know the war's over; I know you aren't here under orders. No—you're trying to orbit in on my landing pattern! I've life—life itself—right here." He loosed his hold on the orb with one hand and flung palm out in a florid gesture. "Everything a tech could want! And it's mine—to have forever." He giggled again, and that sound following the coolness of his words was an erratic break to frighten a man who had witnessed many crack-ups at Rehab.

"Forever!" Dean repeated. "That's it—why, you're trying to planet in! You want it, too! Live forever with every power in your hand when you reach for it." The fingers of his outheld hand curled up to form a cup. "Only a tech got here first, and the tech knows what to do and how to do it. You're not the first to try to take over—but you're easy. I know just how to deal with your kind." He fingered the sphere, and Hosteen choked as the stass field squeezed in upon his throat.

"I could crush you flat, nature boy, just as flat as an insect under a boot sole. Only—that would be a stupid waste. My friends below—they like amusement. They'll have you to play with."

The stranger touched a circlet fitting in a tight band,

about his throat. Then he called aloud, and his shout was the twittering whistle of a Norbie.

Hosteen watched the tunnel entrance behind Dean. "Now!" He thought that order.

A flash of yellow out of the dark and the full force of Surra's weight struck true on Dean's shoulders. His whistle ended in a shriek as he fell. The stass sphere rolled out of his hand, but before the now free Hosteen could seize it, it hit against a rock and bowled over the rim of the ledge to vanish below.

"Do not kill!" Hosteen gave his command as man and cat rolled back and forth across the stone. He moved in on the melee, his limbs stiff, numb, almost as numb as his hand had been after his experience with the alien door lock.

Surra spat, squalled, broke her hold, pawing at her eyes. Dean, yammering still in the Norbie voice, made another throwing motion, and the cat retreated. He looked up at Hosteen, and his face was a devil's mask of open, insane rage. With a last cry he headed for the tunnel as Hosteen tackled him. The Amerindian's cramped limbs brought him down too short; his fingers closed about a leg, but with a vicious kick Dean freed himself and vanished into the passage, the pound of his boots sounding back as he ran.

Surra was still pawing at her eyes. Hosteen grasped a handful of loose hair and skin on her shoulders and pulled her to him. The Norbies Dean had summoned could not be far away. There was only one retreat from this ledge—back into the mountain after Dean. He hoped that some taboo would keep the natives from nosing after.

A head crowned with black horns rose into sight. The

Norbie attacked in a scuttling rush, knife in hand. Then Hosteen was fighting for his life just within the passage entrance. He forced heavy feet and hands into the tricks of unarmed combat that had been a part of his Commando training, rolling farther into the dark, his opponent following.

Pain scored a hot slash along Hosteen's side as the heart thrust the other had aimed missed. He pulled loose and brought down his hand on the native's neck just above the collar bone. As the Norbie fell back with a choking gasp, Hosteen pried the knift hilt out of his hand.

There was a whir in the air, and an arrow cut the frawn fabric of the torn shirt at the Terran's shoulder. On his hands and knees, Hosteen scrambled back, hearing Surra's whining complaint as she went ahead. There was more than one archer taking aim now into the tunnel. He could see the arcs of their bows against the daylight. But the odd dark that blanketed the Sealed Cave workings was his protection. Keeping low, he escaped the arrows flying overhead, and none of the natives ventured in—he had been right about the taboo.

When he judged that a turn in the passage cloaked him from feathered death, Hosteen paused, snapped on his torch, and called Surra to him. What Dean had done to the cat Hosteen did not know. Her eyes were watering and she was in distress, but Hosteen's simple tests confirmed the fact that her sight was not affected and that she was already beginning to recover.

But Surra's ire was fully aroused, and she was determined to trail Dean— which agreed with Hosteen's desire. He wanted to catch up with the renegade tech. And with a knife now in his belt sheath and a better understanding of the man he hunted, the odds were no longer all in the other's favor, though reason told the Terran that a length of metal, well wrought and deadly as it was, was no defense against the bag of tricks the tech might have ready.

The dune cat padded on with confidence. She knew where she was going. Only that did not last. In a stretch of tunnel where there was no break in the wall, Surra stopped short, then circled slowly about, sniffing at the flooring, before, completely baffled, she vented her disappointment in a squall such as she would give upon missing an easy kill.

Hosteen beamed the torch at the floor, more than half expecting to see one of the spiral and dot inlays there. But there was no such path here, no band of bulbs on the wall to open one of those weird other-dimension doors. This was simply another secret of the passages that Dean knew—to the bafflement of his enemies.

Could the tech come and go from any part of the caverns at his will? Or were there "stations" from which one could make such journeys? Hosteen wished now that he had investigated more closely the place into which he had dropped when he had used Dean's door on the platform.

There was nothing to do now but wander through the passages in hope of finding such a door or return to the surface, where he did not doubt he would find the Norbies waiting. How had Surra come into the mountain—by another tunnel?

The Terran squatted down and called the cat to him. With his hand on her head, he strove to have her recall her entrance into the passages.

Those very attributes that made her so effectively a part of the team worked against him now. Surra had been thoroughly aroused by Dean's counter to her attack. She had put out of mind everything but her desire to run him down. And now she was interested only in that and not in what seemed to her to be meaningless inquiries about the passages. The patience Hosteen had always used in dealing with the team held, in spite of his wish for action.

Dean—free in these burrows to use the knowledge of the installations. And Logan— When Hosteen thought of Logan, it was like the burn of a blaster ray across his flesh. The one small hope the Terran clung to was the tube on the board that had lighted. Even if Logan had not arrived in the big hall, he might have escaped the death of the Dry day and be wandering elsewhere in this maze.

"Baku—Gorgol." Since Surra would not respond to Hosteen's first questions, he tried a more oblique approach. And now her concentration on Dean was shaken.

"High—up." As always the answers were not clear. Human mind groped to find a better touch with feline.

"Up—where?" the Beast Master urged.

There was a moment of withdrawal. Was Surra refusing, as she could do upon occasion? Then the cat's head moved under Hosteen's hand, and her muzzle raised as if drawing from the air some message he could not hope to read.

"That one is gone for now—but we shall hunt him," Hosteen promised. "But to so hunt, the team is needed. Where is Baku?"

That had made the right impression. Too long they had been tied together; they both needed the security of that relationship.

Surra made no answer but pulled out of his touch and

started down the passage with some of the same determination she had displayed in the trailing of Dean.

No man could ever have traced his way through the labyrinth where Surra now played guide. They went from passage to passage, bypassed caves and chambers where evidence of the aliens was present in installations, fittings, and objects whose purpose Hosteen could not grasp in a glance or two and which interested Surra not at all. However, the cat appeared to know just where she was going and why.

Their way had led down and up again so many times that Hosteen was bewildered, though he came to believe that they were no longer under the same mountain. Finally, Surra cut out on one of the worked tunnels where the walls were black coated and came into a cleft of bare, untooled rock. Here man had to take cat's path on his hands and knees.

There was a last narrow crevice through which Hosteen crawled to light, air, and the fresh scent of growing things—a small valley into which the Big Dry had not ventured any more than it did into that of the native village. Hosteen sat down wearily to look about.

Now that he had a chance to study the vegetation, he saw a difference. This was a green-green world—not yellow-green, nor red-green, nor brown-green—as the vegetation of Arzor was elsewhere. And where had he ever seen foliage such as that of a small bush a hand's distance away?

A thunderbolt swooped down on black wings from the sky! Baku settled on the ground and came toward the Beast Master, her wings half spread, uttering a series of piercing cries. And the warmth of her greeting was part of their belonging.

But when her clamor was echoed by a sharp whistle from the bushes, Hosteen tensed, his hand going to his knife. That Norbie signal had come to mean danger.

Surra stretched out in a patch of open sunlight, blinking her eyes, giving no alarm. As Hosteen got to his feet, Gorgol came into the open. The young Norbie showed some damage. A poultice of crushed leaves was tied in a netting of grass stems about his left forearm, and there was a purple bruise mottling that side of his face, swelling the flesh until he could see only through a slit of eye. The threads knotting his yoris-tooth breastplate together had broken, and a section was missing.

"Storm!" he signed, and then put out his hand, drawing finger tips lightly down the Terran's arm as if he needed the assurance of touch to accept the other's appearance.

Baku had taken to the air, then settled down again on Hosteen's shoulder. And he braced himself under her weight as she dipped her head to put that beak, which could be such a lethal weapon, against his cheek in quick caress.

"Where are we?" Hosteen glanced at the mountain crests reared to the sky about the pocket of earth that held them. He did not recognize any of them, could not have told in which direction their tunnel wandering had brought them.

"In the mountains," Gorgol signed, an explanation that did not explain at all. "We ran far before the fires."

"We?"

Gorgol turned his head and pursed his lips for another whistle. For a moment Hosteen hoped Logan had found his way here too. But the man coming out of a screen of lacy fronds was a stranger.

Rags of green uniform still slung to a lath-thin body, a body displaying dark bruises such as Gorgol bore. Only it was a human body, and there were no horns, only a mop of brown hair on the head.

"So—Zolti was right," the stranger said in a voice that shook a little. "There was help here all along—we could have made it out—home."

Then he was on the ground as if his long legs had folded bonelessly under him, his face buried in his scratched and earth-streaked hands, his sharp shoulder blades shaking with harsh, tearing sobs he could not control.

SIXTEEN

"Who is this one?" Hosteen asked Gorgol.

"I do not know, for he has not the finger talk," the native signed in return. "We came together on the mountain, and he led me on a path through the flames. I think that he is one who has run in fear for long and long, and yet still will fight—truly a warrior."

Hosteen signaled with a twitch of shoulder, and Baku took off for a perch on a nearby rock. The Terran sat down beside the stranger and laid his hand gently on the bowed back.

"Who are you, friend?" He used the Galactic basic of the Service, but he was not greatly surprised when broken words came in Terran.

"Najar, Mikki Najar, Reconnaissance scout—500th Landing force."

His voice had steadied. Now he dropped his hands and turned his head to face Hosteen directly, a puzzled expression on his features as he continued to study the Amerindian.

"Hosteen Storm, Beast Master," Hosteen identified himself and then added, "The war is over, you know."

Najar nodded slowly. "I know. But this is a holdout planet, isn't it? That's why you're here—or is that wrong, too?"

"This is Arzor, a frontier settlement world. We had an Xik holdout pocket, yes, but cleaned it up months ago. And it was only one shipload of Xiks. Most of them blew themselves up when they tried to take off. I'm not here as a soldier—this is my home now."

There were bitter lines about Najar's mouth. "Just some more of Dean's lies. You're Terran, aren't you?"

Hosteen nodded and then added, "Arzoran now. I've taken up land in the plains—"

"And this *is* a Confederacy settlement planet not an Xik world?"

"Yes."

"For how long?"

"Over two hundred Terran years anyway—second and third generations from First Ship families are holding lands now. You came in on the LB?"

"Yes." Najar's bitterness had reached his voice now. "Lafdale was a pilot, and he was a good one—got us down without smashing up. Then we walked out straight into a native attack. They didn't kill us—might have been better if they had—just herded us up the mountainside and put us in a cave. We lost Lafdale in an underground place full of water. He was pulled off a wharf there by something big—something we never really saw. Then"—Najar shook his head slowly from side to side—"it was a kind of nightmare. Roostav—he went missing; we never found him—that was in a cave full of broken walls. Dean kept urging us on. He was excited, said we were on to something big. And Zolti—he'd been a Hist-tech before the war—he said that this was a settled planet and we could find help if we could get back to the LB com. We never knew if the signals we sent at landing had ever been picked up. But Dean talked him down, said he knew where we were—right in the territory where the Xik had holdouts all over—that the hostile attitude of the natives proved we were in an Xik influence zone."

He paused and rubbed his hand across his face. "The other two of us, Widders and I, we didn't know what to think. Dean and Zolti, they were the big brains. Both of them said we were in a place where there was something big from the old times. And Dean—we were all out of Rehab, you know." He glanced almost furtively at Hosteen.

"For all Terrans there was Rehab—afterwards," the Amerindian replied soberly.

"Well, Dean, he—somehow he didn't want to go back, back to the way he had had it before the war, I mean. He'd been pretty important in the Service, and he liked that. Maybe he was able to cover up in Rehab, but after we landed here he was a different person, excited, alive. Then he just took over, ran us— He kept insisting it was our duty to learn all we could about this place, use it against the Xiks. And he swore Zolti was mistaken, that we had been off course of any settler planet when we dropped here.

"Then we found the place of the path." Again Najar stopped and Hosteen thought he was trying to pick words to explain something he did not understand himself.

"You found this?" The Terran sketched with a finger tip in the dust the spiral and dot.

"Yes. You must have seen it too!"

"And followed it."

"Dean said it was a way out. I don't know how he knew that. He picked information out of the air—or so it seemed. One minute he'd be as puzzled as we were; then all at once he'd explain—and he'd be right! Funny though, he didn't want to try that path first. Zolti did— walked around and around—then he just wasn't there!

"Widders, he was out of his head a little by then. Kept saying over and over that things hid behind rocks to watch us. He threw stones into every shadow. When Zolti went like that, Widders started screaming. He ran around and around the coil, hit the center—and then was gone—

"Dean took the same orbit. And I—well, I wasn't going to stay there alone. So I did it—ended up in a three-cornered box."

"You saw the hall of the machines?" Hosteen asked.

"Yes. Dean was there. And he was crazy-wild, running up and down, patting them and talking to himself about how all this was the place he had been meant to find— that the voices in his head had told him and that now he held the whole world right in his hand. Listening to him was like being back in Rehab in the early days. I hid out and watched him. Then he ended up in a corner where there was a big hoop—got inside that and lay down on the floor, curled up as if he were asleep. There was a light and noise—I couldn't watch—something queer happened to your eyes when you tried to. So I went to hunt Widders and Zolti. Only, if they came that way, they were gone again. I didn't see them—not then."

"But you did later?"

"Maybe—one. Only nobody could be sure—just bones that looked fresh." Najar's eyes closed, and Hosteen felt the shudder that shook his wasted body. "I didn't stay *there* to hunt. Somehow I found this valley outside—"

He looked around, gratitude mirrored in his eyes.

"It was wonderful, after all those other places, to be out in the open with things—real things—growing, almost like home. And there was a way higher up to get out—down to where the natives were. I watched them. Then all at once more and more of them kept coming, and I guessed Dean was up to something. Thunder and lightning—not the normal kind— I tried to find out what was going on, mapped some of the ways in and out—"

"You didn't think of trying to contact Dean again?"

Najar's gaze dropped to his hands. "No—I didn't. You may think that's queer, Storm. But Dean, he'd been changing all the time since we landed here. And when I saw him so wild in that hall—well, I didn't want to have anything to do with him again. He was raving about being picked to rule a world—it was enough to make you think you were crazy, too. I didn't want any part of him."

Hosteen agreed. The man he had fronted at the tunnel mouth had been removed from human kind, unreachable, unless a trained psycho-tech could find a channel to connect Dean again with the world.

"I'm pretty good at trailing"—Najar's ordinary flat tone now held a spark of pride—"being a Recon scout, and I got around so that the natives didn't suspect me. Of course, not many of them ever came far up the mountain, and when they did, they kept to paths. Then I saw a 'copter come over, and it was one of ours! That made Dean's story about an Xik world nonsense, and I thought maybe our boys had moved in and cleaned up.

"So I went down to signal it. There was a flash just after the 'copter set down, and that fire cut around the whole landing area. I couldn't get to it until afterwards—there was a dead man there, and all the rest burned up. And I'd been counting a lot on getting out—" Again he stared at his hands. "I was sick, straight through to my insides, sick enough to get at Dean. So I took to the mountain passages, hoping to meet him. Got to the machine hall twice, only he was never there. You don't have any idea, Storm, about how big this digging really is—passages running through the mountains and under them, all sorts of caverns and rooms. I've seen things—strictly unhealthy." Again shudders ran through him. "Sometimes I wondered if I weren't as crazy as Dean—else I wouldn't be seeing some of those things.

"But I never caught up with Dean—not until the night there was another fire along the mountain. And I saw this native here beating it ahead of the fire with a big cat and a bird swooping along over them. Dean was watching them come upslope, and he was aiming a tube at them. I cut in and signaled the native into a gap, and the cat and bird came along. The gap led in here, then—"

"Then?" Hosteen asked.

"Then," Najar reiterated grimly, his features set, "one of those tame lightning bolts smashed down just as we were almost through it—sealed us in with a landslide and knocked us around some so we weren't much use for days afterwards. Lucky there's water in here and some fruit— The bird tried to get out, but the way it acted made you think there was some kind of lid up there over this whole

193

place. Then one day the cat was gone, and we guessed she'd found a way out. We've been hunting for that ever since. Now you know it all—"

"Yes," Hosteen replied somewhat absently. One piece of Najar's story was enlightening—all of the survivors' party had left the spiral path in the valley at the same time, but apparently not all had landed at the same terminal in the big hall when that beyond-time-and-space journey was completed. Logan—had Logan come out at some other point in the mountain maze? Hosteen turned upon Najar now with a sharpness born of renewed hope.

"There's a way out—do you think you could find your way back to the hall once you were in the tunnels again?"

"I don't know—I honestly don't know."

Hosteen signed to Gorgol across the castaway's hunched shoulders.

"There is no way across the heights?"

"We can look but we cannot go. Come and see for yourself," the Norbie responded.

They went on a rough scramble up the slope in which was the rock crevice of Surra's door. Then they walked a ledge, which ended in a vast pile of debris.

"The mountain fell—" Gorgol indicated the slip. "And from here one can look—"

Another tricky bit of climbing and they could indeed look—a prospect that was enough to leave one giddy. Down—down—a drop no length of rope on Arzor, Hosteen thought, could dangle to touch bottom. And beyond that crack in the earth, well within sight but as far removed from them as if it existed on another world, uplands sere and baked under that sun, which on their side was so abnormally gentle. A window on the outer world but no door.

Swiftly Hosteen signed the facts he had learned in his explorations and what Najar had told him. Gorgol watched the Terran's fingers with a growing expression of resolution.

"If Ukurti says that this is an ill thing," Gorgol's own hands replied, "then will Krotag and those who ride with Krotag listen, for Ukurti is one having wisdom, and always we have hearkened to his drum. To say that one with a twisted mind is using things left by Those-Who-Have-Gone to make him great—that, too, one can believe. And this is true—if he is known to be one who steals from the past to give himself power, then will the tribes turn from him and listen no more to his drumming."

"But how may it be proved that he is such a one? And do we have the time?" Hosteen countered. "Already he drums raids for the plains. And once there is even one such foray, there will be war—war without truce between your people and mine. Always there have been those among my kind who have mistrusted yours."

"That is true." Gorgol's fingers made an emphatic sign of agreement. "And once the war arrow is sped, who can recall it to the quiver? But there is also this—outside this place lies the hand of the Dry. Water secrets we have, but not enough to sustain any large parties through the Peaks. And those who so venture cannot so do in straight lines but must go from one hidden spring to another, using much time. Were men to march today, it would be"—he spread out his fingers, curled them back into his palms, and opened them out again three times—"these many suns before they would reach the plains."

"Would Krotag listen to you?" Hosteen demanded.

"I am a warrior with scars. In the voice of the clan, I have my speech right. He would listen."

"Then if we can get out of here, get you on the other side of the mountain where you can meet with Krotag and Ukurti—?"

Gorgol stared past Hosteen into the brilliance of the parched land beyond. "Krotag would listen—and beyond Krotag stands Kustig of the Yoris totem, and beyond Kustig, Dankgu of the Xoto standard."

"And if all those listened, the Shosonna would break their peace poles and have no part of this?"

"It might be so. And if the Shosonna marched, then would follow the Warpt of the north and perhaps the Gouskla of the coasts—"

"Splitting Dean's army right down the middle!" Hosteen took fire, but Gorgol's expression was still a sober frown.

"With truce poles broken, there might be another kind of war, for these wild men of the Blue are tied to the medicine here and will fight to uphold it."

"Unless Dean can be proved a false Drummer—"

"Yes. And here are two trails." Gorgol turned away from the "window." "I must find the place of the Zamle totem and you this one who is of your people but a doer of evil."

"And to do those things, we must have a way back through the mountain," Hosteen added.

They held a council of war in the green heart of the valley, Najar, Hosteen, and Gorgol sitting together, Baku and Surra nearby. Storm translated between Gorgol and the off-world veteran as they pooled what knowledge they had of the inner ways. And Najar thought he might be able to guide them to the village side of the heights if he could reach a mid-point within that he had located during his own wanderings. They ate of the fruit from bush and tree, and Hosteen slept, his head pillowed against Surra's furry side, the soft purring of the cat lulling him into a deeper and more restful slumber than any he had known since he left the plains to begin this wild adventure.

It was dark when Gorgol awakened him, and they went to the hole beneath the rock, which was Surra's private exit from the valley. Baku objected with a scream of anger when Hosteen called her to push through with them, and he had to wheedle her into furling wings and taking a footway. Only his firm statement that he and Surra were leaving not to return and that she would remain alone finally brought the eagle to obey, though fierce clicks of her beak made very plain her opinion of the whole maneuver as they crept back through the crack.

Baku settled on Hosteen's shoulder once they reached the passage, her eyes like harsh sparks in the light of the torch. Surra took the lead, setting a gliding pace that brought the men to a fast walk.

The cat was retracing the way by which she had brought Hosteen in, but long before they reached the place where Dean had vanished into thin air, Najar uttered an exclamation and caught at the Beast Master's arm.

"Here!" He was looking alertly about him with the air of a man who had come across some landmark. "This is the way—"

Hosteen recalled Surra, and the party turned into a side tunnel, Najar was now leading. To Hosteen, one of these unmarked passages was much like another, but he knew that just as he had been trained and conditioned to be the leader of a team, so had the Reconnaissance scouts been selected, trained, and psycho-indoctrinated for their service as pathfinders and "first-in" men.

Najar displayed no hesitation as he threaded from one way to another and crossed several small caverns with the certainty of one treading a well-defined trail. Then they stood in a hollow space and saw near its roof a slit of light. Najar pointed to that.

"Opening made by a landslide. This place is a natural cave and opens on the mountainside."

Hosteen had his hand on the first hold to climb to that door when he heard an odd cry from Najar. He half turned and saw the other's face illuminated in the torch Gorgol held. The scout was glaring at Hosteen, his eyes pure hate as he flung himself at the Beast Master, the momentum of his body jamming Storm against the cave wall.

The Amerindian strove to roll his head and his shoulders to avoid blows he knew were meant to kill. Then the torchlight snapped off, and they were in the dark.

"You dirty Xik liar!" Najar spat almost in Hosteen's face. "Liar—!"

He was choked off in mid-breath, his body jerked away from Hosteen's. Gasping, holding his arm where one of those nerve deadening blows had landed, the Beast Master leaned limply against the rock. A furred body pressed against his leg. He reached down, took the torch from Surra's mouth, and snapped it on.

Gorgol stood, his arm crooked about Najar's throat, the

Terran castaway hugged back to the native's chest, his struggles growing weaker as the Norbie exerted pressure on his windpipe.

"Don't kill him!" Hosteen ordered.

Gorgol's grip loosened. He let the off-worlder collapse against him. He transferred his hold to the other's arms, keeping him upright to confront the man he had attacked.

"Why?" Hosteen asked, rubbing feeling back into his arm.

"You said—settler world—no Xik—war over here—" Najar might be helpless in Gorgol's prisoning hand, but his spirit—and his hate—were unbeaten. "There's a recon-broadcaster out there!"

Hosteen stared at him blankly—not that he doubted Najar's word or now wondered at the other's reaction. A Recon scout had an induced sensitivity to certain beamed waves, a homing device that was implanted in him through surgery and hypnotic conditioning. If Najar had caught a recon-beam, he would not be mistaken. But to Hosteen's knowledge the nearest recon-broadcaster was at Galwadi or the Port. Unless—unless Kelson or some other authority was moving into the Blue!

"I told you the truth," he said. "But—maybe—maybe we're already too late. The Patrol could have been called in."

SEVENTEEN

"To the west—there—" Najar's right hand was a compass direction, pointing southwest.

Baku—Hosteen thought the command that sent the eagle up and out into the sky. She soared past the point of their sighting, exulting, in the freedom she had not been able to find in the invisibly roofed valley. And from her came the report he wanted.

There was a party of men, encamped in a hollow, doubtless digging in for protection against the heat of the day. Now Hosteen depended upon Gorgol for advice.

"Can we reach them before the sun is too high?"

The Norbie was uncertain. And Hosteen could give him little help as to distance, though Najar insisted from the strength of the recon-beam the camp could not be farther than five miles. Only, five miles in this broken country for men on foot might be equal to half a day's journey in the plains.

"If these others come into the Blue," Gorgol warned, "then will all of my people unite against them, and there will be no hope of breaking truce between tribe and tribe."

"That is so. But if you go to the clans and I and this one who knows much concerning the evil one go to the settlers, then with our talk we may hold them apart until the war arrows can be hidden and wise heads stand up in council."

Gorgol climbed to the top of the rocky pile hiding the cave entrance, studying a southern route. His fingers moved.

"For me the way is not hard; for you it may be impossible. The choice is yours."

"What about it?" Hosteen asked Najar. "They'll have to hole up during the day. But they'll be moving on. And they have scouts out in this territory or you wouldn't have picked up that beam. And once they enter the big valley, there'll be a fight for sure—one that Dean will win under the present circumstances and that will begin his war."

"What will you do?" Najar counterquestioned.

"Try to reach them before night when they'll move on—"

Perhaps that was the wrong decision; perhaps his place was here, pursuing Dean through the interior burrows. But even if some miracle of luck would put the renegade tech into his hands, there would still be war when the off-world force crossed the line into the Blue.

"You'll never find them unless you follow the beam." Najar rubbed the back of his hand across his mouth.

"I have Baku and Surra," Hosteen replied, though in one way Najar was right. With the Recon scout they could take the quickest and easiest route to that camp, following the broadcast.

Najar hitched the cord of a canteen around his bony shoulder. "We'd better blast if we're going." He circled the rocks and started on.

Hosteen waved a hand at Gorgol, and the Norbie slid down the other side of the rock pile, heading into the valley to find the clansmen who might listen to him if they were not provoked by an invasion.

It was still early enough so that the heat was no more than that of midmorning in the milder season. Hosteen, eying the sun's angle, thought they might squeeze in two or two and a half hours of travel before they would have to lay up. Then they might have another hour—if they were lucky—in the early evening. But the best way was to think only of what lay immediately ahead—first of the next ridge or crevice, then, as the sun burnt higher and patches of shade were few, of the next ten steps, five steps, ahead.

Surra, ranging wider than the men, disappeared, only keeping mental contact with Hosteen. The time came when he asked of her the location of a hiding hole, for the time between their rests grew shorter and the land beyond was as barren and sun-seared as that he had seen through the "window" in the sealed valley wall.

Najar took a quick step farther right.

"The beam—it has doubled its strength! We're either practically on top of them or there's an emergency recall." From their careful, slow plod he broke into a trot, topping a small ravine and dropping into it in a cascade of rocks and earth. At the same time Surra's alert came—she had sighted the camp.

The ravine fed them into a larger break, and there they came upon a halt station such as Norbies and hunters used in the Peaks—a collection of stones heaped over a pit in the earth—in which men could rest during the day in a livable atmosphere. Surra prowled about its circumference and raised her voice in a growl of feline exasperation.

Hosteen hurried on and clawed at the frawn-skin robe wet down with seal seam to close the entrance. A moment later the head and shoulders of a man pushed that aside—Kelson!

"Storm! We knew you were on the way—Baku came in a few minutes ago. Come in, man, come in. And you, Logan—" Then the Peace Officer took a closer look at Hosteen's companion.

"That isn't Logan—"

"No." Hosteen shoved Najar ahead of him through the hole as Kelson retreated to give them passage. Then Surra and finally he dropped in. He stood there allowing his eyes to adjust to the gloom.

The quarters had been chosen well, the scooped out pit leading back into a cave of sorts. Only Hosteen had little time to assess his surroundings, for he was facing Brad Quade.

"Logan—?"

The question Hosteen had been asking himself for what seemed now to be days of time was put into words—and by the one he most dreaded hearing it from. All he had beside the bare fact of their parting on that strange transport device of the caves was Najar's story of the other man who had taken that route but had not come to the installation hall. If Logan were still alive, he was lost somewhere in the tunnels.

"I don't know—"

"You were with him?"

"Yes—for a while—"

"Storm"—Kelson's hand on his shoulder brought him partly around to face the other—"we picked up that com cast from in there, the one you sent."

All Hosteen's frustration, fears, and fatigue boiled over into rage.

"Then why in the name of the Dang Devil are you heading in? Take one step into that valley and the rocket goes up for sure!" He was shaking. The anger in him, against this country, against the odds of ever pulling down Dean, against the tricks of the cave passages he could not hope to master, was eating at him until he wanted to scream out as loudly as Surra did upon occasion. And now the cat snarled from the shadows and Baku voiced a cry, both of them sensitive to his loss of control.

Two hands on his shoulders now forced him down, steadily but gently. He tried to twist out of that grip and discovered that his tired body would not obey him. Then there was a cup at his cracked lips, and he drank thirstily until it was removed.

"Listen, boy, no one is trying to run this through blind. We've scouts in the heights, but they have orders not to go into that Valley. Can you give us some idea of what is going on?" Quade spoke quietly as he settled Hosteen on the floor of their sunhide, moistened a cloth in a milky liquid he had poured from a small container, and with it patted Hosteen's face, throat, and chest. The aromatic scent of the stuff brought with it soothing if fleeting memories of relaxing at the day's end back at the holding.

The younger man was as sobered as if in the heat of

his anger he had plunged into an icy stream. And in terse sentences he told them what little he knew, then waved Najar forward to add his part of the tale.

"You're right," Kelson commented when they were done. "Dean is the answer. An unstable tech with a genius-level brain turned loose in a Sealed Cave storehouse— Lord, that could finish Arzor just as quickly as a continental Tri-X bomb!"

"You've called the Patrol in?" Hosteen asked.

"Not officially yet. We've borrowed some trained personnel. Maybe now"—he stood up in the dugout, his hands on his hips, his face flushed with more than the heat of their shelter—"the Council will listen to a little common sense. This country should have been adequately patrolled five, ten years ago."

"Intrusion of treaty rights," Quade reminded.

"Treaty rights! Nobody's suggesting we curtail Norbie treaty rights—at least I'm not, though you'd have a different answer from some of those in the Peaks. No! I want—just as I have always wanted—a local force of Norbie-cum-settler to police the outback. That's what we needed from the first—could have had it last year if you taxpayers had pushed for it. Such a corps would have routed out that Xik gang before they dug in—and they could have stopped this before it even started. You say now this Ukurti is against Dean's war talk and he can carry his clan Chief with him. Well, we could get the good will of natives of that type and their backing. That's not breaking any treaty rights I know of—but no, that's too simple for those soft-sitting Galwadi pets. Now it may be too late. If we are forced to call in the Patrol to handle Dean—"

He did not have to continue. They all knew what that would mean—a loss of settler and Norbie independence, a setting up of off-world control for an indefinite period, the end to native growth, which was their hope for the future.

"How long do we have before the authorities will move?" Hosteen asked.

"How long will Dean hold off on his raids?" Kelson barked. "If our scouts report any parties of warriors leaving the Blue and we don't have the power to stop them—"

"Power," repeated Hosteen softly. "Dean's control in there rests on the fact the natives believe it's true medicine. I think there was a residue of some alien knowledge among the Norbies of the Blue—some of those machines must have been left running. There is certainly weather control in the village valley and the smaller one where Najar hid out. Perhaps the Norbies were able to make use of other devices—we saw the village Drummer pull a trick that certainly never originated on Arzor—without understanding them. Then Dean has activated more, so he's a part of the medicine, which makes him taboo and a man of power—"

"And the answer is—remove Dean?" Kelson speculated.

"Not remove him," Quade cut in, and Hosteen nodded agreement. "That would merely add to the medicine—were he to disappear. And if he is removed bodily and that action discovered, it would be a declaration of war. He has to be removed by those who set him up."

"No chance of that that I can see," Kelson exploded.

"Ukurti's attitude is in our favor," Quade pointed out.

"And Dean is unstable. We have to get at him on a ground he believes is safe—"

Hosteen stirred. "In the mountain!"

"That's right—in the mountain."

"It's a tangle of passages. To find him in there, when he knows those interdimension transports and we don't—" Hosteen could see the futility of such a chase, and yet that was their only chance. If they could actually capture Dean, hold him prisoner in the taboo mountain where his native allies would not venture, they would have time to work out a method of unmasking him.

"Najar." Quade spoke to the castaway. "You can find that installation hall?"

"I can try. But as Storm says, that's a mighty big mountain or mountains, and there're a lot of passages. It's easy to get lost—"

"We can take off as soon as it cools this evening," Kelson began briskly.

"*We* take off—you stay here and contact the rest of the force," Quade corrected. "No, don't try to finger me down over this, Jon. You're official, and you can swing weight with those rocket boys back in the lowlands. How much do you think they'd listen to me? I'm just another rider scrabbling up a frawn herd as far as they're concerned. Najar," he asked, "are you willing to give us a trail leading back in there?"

The castaway looked down at the ground. As well as if he had said it aloud, Hosteen could guess what the other wanted to reply, that he had finally won free of the nightmare in which he had been encased since the crash landing in the Blue. Najar had a good chance now of completing that interrupted voyage, of getting home. But

207

he was Terran—for him, too, no home world was waiting. Was it that loss that tipped the scales in their favor?

"All right." He wiped his hands across the tatters that served him as a shirt. "Only I make no promises about finding your man."

"That's understood. Anyway—we can fit you out."

Kelson energetically tackled the packs stored at the back of the sunhide, rummaging through supplies meant to equip a scout post. There were arms to be had, stunners, belt knives, fresh clothing, supplies of energy tablets.

Hosteen slept away most of that day. Since his initial inquiry, Quade had not spoken of Logan, but the thought of him was there, and Logan himself walked through Hosteen's troubled dreams. At nightfull he awoke sweating, from a vivid return to the transport wedge in the valley—from which, in that nightmare, he had seen Logan vanish, knowing that he had no way of following after, the reversal of what had actually happened. And now the Amerindian could not understand his earlier action. When he had had that compulsion to walk the spiral, why had he not called Logan, made the other do likewise? Why had he been so buried in concentrated effort that he had ignored his half-brother? He could find no excuse—none at all.

Baku was left with Kelson, with orders to keep liaison between the scout post and the mountainside. The eagle hated the tunnels, and her particular gifts were useless there. But Surra sped with the party, backtracking the route that had brought them there that morning.

Once again within the cave, Hosteen put his arm about the cat. In his hold he could feel the play of her powerful shoulder muscles. Just as she had known his frustrated anger back in the hide-up, so did she now react to the job ahead. They had a mission and one in which time itself was drawing the war arrow against them.

"Find—find!" He projected a mental picture of Dean, urged it upon Surra with all the clarity and force he could muster.

Hosteen felt as well as heard the deep growl that vibrated through her as might the purr of a more contented moment. He did not know whether her feline hunting sense would bring them any nearer their quarry. Luck—or "medicine"—could still play a part in this blind hunt. Over Surra's body he looked to Najar in an appeal that was also part order.

"Can you guide us to any main passage from here?"

"Most of 'em are main passages as far as I know." The other did not sound optimistic, but he took the lead, and they started on into the heart of the mountain.

Here Surra showed no desire to roam ahead; instead, she matched her pace to Hosteen's as well as four feet could match two. He was alert to her always, relying more upon the cat than upon Najar's ability to bring them into a section where they might hope to encounter Dean, so he knew instantly when the cat paused, even before she swung half across his path to half him.

Quade, knowing of old how Surra operated, stopped, and Najar looked around, puzzled, and then impatient.

"What's the—?" He had out only half the question when Hosteen signaled him to silence.

Surra's actions were the same as the time when Dean had vanished in that other tunnel. And the Amerindian was certain that this must be another of the mysterious transfer points.

The cat's head was cocked slightly to one side, and her whole stance pictured the act of listening—listening to something their dull human ears could not pick up. Without moving more than his hands, Hosteen switched his torch on to full beam, played that bank of light in a careful sweep over the floor under them and the right wall. But there were no spiral markings such as he had more than half hoped to sight. The beam went to his left and again revealed unmarked surface.

Yet Surra was still listening. Then the cat arose on her hind feet, her muzzle pointed up—as if she scented what she had heard.

Overhead! Not under foot as it had been in the valley, but overhead! Hosteen flashed his torch straight up. But how could that pattern he had come to know be followed upside down?

"That it?" Quade asked.

"Yes. Only I don't see—" Hosteen began, and then suddenly he did. Just as he had been pushed by a compulsion he did not understand to walk the spiral in the valley wedge, so here an order outside of his consciousness brought his hand up over his head to touch the open end of the spiral. Only this time he fought that pull, fought it enough to keep his awareness of those with him.

"I think—" It was hard to speak, to be able to keep his mind off the tracing of that pattern with his finger tips. The urgency to do so was like pain, racing from finger tips to flood his whole body. "We must do this," he said at last.

A furred body pressed against his. Surra! Surra who had no hand to trace for her. To go would be deserting Surra. His other hand groped along that furred back after he passed the torch to Quade. He could no longer turn his eyes away from that pattern, which glowed in his mind as well as on the stone overhead.

Hosteen thought of the pattern and took a grip on the loose skin at the back of the cat's neck, beginning to walk around and around with the fingers of his other hand tracing the roof spiral he had to go on tiptoe to touch. Surra was following his pull without complaint, around— around— Now! His finger tip was on the dot—

Dark—and the terror of that journey through the dark, the red spark that was Curra and a white-yellow one that was Hosteen Storm in company still—

Light around him. Hosteen put out a hand to steady his body and felt the sleek chill of metal. He was back on the dais of the hall platform while Surra pulled free of his hold and faced down the nearest aisle, her mouth wrinkled in a soundless snarl of menace.

EIGHTEEN

Hosteen drew his stunner. From the cat came knowledge that his less acute human senses could not supply. Down those rows of machines there was a hunt in progress, and the hunted was friend, not enemy. Gorgol—successful in obtaining allies—penetrating to this center of taboo territory? Or—the Terran's grip on the stunner tightened—Logan at last?

Surra leaped from the platform in a distance-covering bound. Then she glided into cover between two installations as Hosteen followed.

Above the hum of the encased machinery Hosteen thought he heard something else—a ticking, more metallic than the drumbeats of the Norbie tambours. He caught up with Surra where she crouched low, intent upon what lay around a corner. The hair along the big cat's spine was roughened; her big ears were folded against her skull. She spat, and one paw arose as if to slash out.

The thing she stalked was unnatural—not alive by her definition of life. Shadow thing—? No! Housteen caught sound of that scuttle. Something flashed with super speed, very close to the ground, from one machine base to the next! No—no shadows this time.

He edged past the cat and then side-stepped just in time to avoid the headlong rush of someone alive—alive and human.

"Logan!" Housteen caught at the other, and an unkempt head turned. Lips were pressed tight to teeth in a snarl akin to Surra's.

A spark of recognition broke in the depths of those too bright eyes, a hand pawed at Housteen's, and Logan swayed forward, for a moment resting his body against his brother's, his heavy breathing close to a sob. Only for a moment, then his head lifted, his eyes widened, and he gasped:

"Hosteen! Behind you!"

Surra squalled, struck out at the thing whipping across the pavement, and recoiled as if flung back. It was a glittering silver ribbon with an almost intelligent aura of malignancy about it, from which a tapering end rose and pointed at the men.

"Get it—quick!" Logan cried.

Hosteen pressed stunner firing button. An eye-searing burst of light came from the snake thing as the beam caught it full on.

"You did it!" The younger man's voice held the ragged edge of hysteria.

"What?"

"A live machine—one of the crawlers—"

Logan loosed his grip on Hosteen and tottered to the metal ribbon. A thin tendril of smoke arose as it battered its length senselessly against the floor. Logan stamped once, grinding his boot heel into the thing.

"I've wanted to do that for hours," he informed Hosteen. "There's more of 'em, though—we'll have to watch out. And"—his gaze shifted to the weapon in Hosteen's fist—"where in the name of the Seven Suns did you get that?"

"We've reinforcements." For the first time Hosteen wondered about that. Would Najar and Quade be able to follow him, or was this another time when one of the baffling spiral paths would deposit travelers at different destinations?

"Listen." He pulled Logan away from the feebly quivering "snake." "Back there in the valley—did you walk the spiral path the same way I did?"

"Sure. You just vanished into air—I had to follow."

"Where did you land?"

"In a place I wouldn't have believed existed—after seeing the rest of this demon-inspired hole. All the time we were muckin' around there was a place in here with regular livin' quarters. But I ran into someone there—an off-worlder who has the run of this whole holdin'. For days—seems like days anyway—he's been runnin' me!" Logan was grimly bitter. "Turned those clockwork snakes loose and left me to it. I slowed up one of 'em with rocks in another cavern like the pen one and pushed one into a river. You took out this one, but there's a pack of 'em—"

"Thief!"

The word boomed out of the air right over their heads, freezing both.

"Hide if you wish." There was condescension in that. "You cannot escape, you know. The crawlers will deliver

214

you to me just as I order. Have you not had enough of running?"

Surra had given no warning. Did Dean have some form of video watching them?

"You waste time in skulking. And a rock—if you have one left—is a poor weapon against this which can deal with a mountain if I so will it."

A bolt of fire flashed over their heads well above the level of the machines.

A rock for a weapon! Then Dean did not know Hosteen had joined Logan! He was not watching them; he was only sure Logan had been hunted into the hall and was hiding out there.

"You would be better advised not to keep me waiting. Either you will come to me now or my pets will be given a full charge and turned loose to use it. You will be given to the count of five to consider the disadvantages of being a dead hero, and then you will come to the platform in this hall. One—two—"

Logan's fingers made sign talk. "I'll go and keep him busy."

"Right. Surra will take the left aisle, I the right. We'll flank you in."

"—three—four—"

Logan walked out into full view of the platform. Two fingers of the hand hanging by his side twitched. Dean was up there waiting.

Hosteen started forward at a pace slightly slower than Logan's. All they had to fear for the present was a sudden appearance of another "snake."

Dean stood with his back to the board, over which rainbow lights ran in tubes. He was plainly pleased with himself. And Hosteen did not doubt he was equipped with a stass bulb or some other alien weapon.

"So the thief does not escape."

"As I told you before, I'm no thief!" Logan retorted with genuine heat. "I was lost here, and I don't know how I got into that room where you found me—"

"Maybe not yet a thief in practice, but in intent, yes. Don't you suppose that I know any man would give years of life to master these secrets. Few ever conceive of such power as this hall holds. I am Lord of Thunder, Master of Lightning in the eyes of the natives—and they are right! This world is mine. It took the combined forces of all twenty solar systems in the Confederacy ten years to put down the Xiks. I was one of the techs sent to study and dismantle their headquarters on Raybo. And we thought we had uncovered secrets then. But they had nothing to compare with the knowledge waiting here. I was chosen to use the teaching tapes stored here, the cramming machines—they were waiting for me, *me* alone, not for stupid little men, ignorant thieves. This is all mine—"

Hosteen quickened pace and checked with Surra by mind touch.

"Why didn't you finish me off with your crawlers or your tame lightin'—if that's the way you feel about it?" Logan was keeping Dean talking. The tech, alone so long, must relish an audience of one of his own race.

"There is plenty of time to finish you off, as you say. I wanted you occupied for a space, kept away from places where you might get into mischief. You could not be allowed to interfere with the plan."

"This plan of yours"—Logan was only a few steps

from the platform—"is to take over Arzor and then branch out. Beat the Xiks at their old game."

"Those who built this place"—Dean was fingering a small ball, another stass broadcaster Hosteen believed; otherwise, the Terran could not see that the other was armed—"had an empire into which all the Xik worlds and the Confederacy could both have been fitted and forgotten. All their knowledge—it is here. They foresaw some blasting end—made this into a storehouse—" He flung out his hand.

Hosteen fired the stunner. That ray should have clipped Dean alongside the head, a tricky shot, and it failed. A breath of the beam must have cut close enough to confuse him momentarily but not enough to put him out. Logan launched himself at the man who was staggering, only to crash heavily, completely helpless in stass, as Dean thumbed his control globe.

The tech was standing directly before the board, and Hosteen dared not try a second shot. A ray touching those sensitive bulbs might create havoc. The Terran signaled Surra.

Out of hiding the cat made a great arching leap that brought her up on the platform, facing Dean. Then she struck some invisible barrier and screamed aloud in anger and fear, as she was flattened to the floor.

Pressed back against the board, Dean reached for a lever, and Hosteen made his own move. Surra, striving still to reach her quarry, was aiming forepaw blows at nothing, and her raging actions held the tech's attention as Hosteen jumped to the platform in turn. But he did not advance on Dean.

Instead, his own hand went out to a bank of those small bulbs that studded the boards in bands.

"Try that"—his warning crackled as if his words held the voltage born in the installations about them—"and I move too!"

Dean's head whipped about. He stared with feral eyes at the Amerindian. Hosteen knew that his threat could be an empty one; now he must depend upon what some men termed luck and his own breed knew as "medicine."

"You fool! There's death there!"

"I do not doubt it," Hosteen assured him. "Better dead men here than raiders loosed on the plains and a dead world to follow." Bold words—a part of him hoped he would not have to prove them.

"Release the stass!" Hosteen ordered. If he could only keep Dean alarmed for just a few seconds!

But the tech did not obey. Hosteen moved his hand closer to the row of bulbs. He thought he felt warmth there, perhaps a promise of fire to come. Then Dean hurled the ball out into the aisle.

"Fool! Get away from that—you'll have the mountain down upon us!"

Hosteen dropped his hand to the butt of the stunner. Now he could ray the other into unconsciousness, and their job would be over.

A breath of air, a sound came from behind him. He jerked his head. Two figures appeared out of nowhere on the dais. Hosteen heard Logan call out and felt a lash of burning heat about his upper arms and chest so that the stunner dropped from helpless fingers.

Dean was away, running, dodging behind one of the cased machines, Surra a tawny streak at his back. Hosteen swayed, then recovered his balance on the very edge of the platform. He saw Surra drop, roll helplessly—Dean must have picked up the stass.

Quade passed Hosteen, running toward the spot where the cat lay. But before him was Logan, scrambling on hands and knees. The younger man paused, and then he threw—with the practised wrist snap of a veteran knife man. There was a cry from beyond.

Hosteen was only half aware of the struggle there. The pain in his arm and shoulder was like a living thing eating his quivering flesh. He dropped down and watched Logan and his father drag a wildly struggling Dean into view. And in Logan's hand was the weapon that had brought the tech down, the now blood-stained horn he had taken from the skull found in the pens.

As they returned, the tubing on the board came to life. The waving line of lavender, which had always showed steady color from the first time Hosteen had seen the hall, was deepening in hue, its added flow of energy clearly visible.

Dean stopped struggling abruptly. A new kind of concentration molded his features. In an instant he had dropped his frenzied fight for freedom and become an alert tech faced by a problem in his own field.

"What is it?" Brad Quade demanded.

Dean shrugged impatiently, as if to throw off both question and the hold that kept him from the platform. "I don't know—"

Najar was beside Hosteen, giving the Amerindian a hand up. No, he had not been wrong, for Surra had caught it too—the warning that was a part of the brilliance in that band of light, as well as a part of man and beast who shared another kind of awareness.

"We must get out of here." Hosteen lurched toward the dais.

Logan, Quade, Najar—three pairs of eyes were on him. Surra was already by his side.

"What is it?" This time Brad Quade asked his stepson and not the tech.

"I don't know!" Hosteen made the same answer. "But we have to get out of here and fast." His inner tension was swelling into panic—such as had dogged him in the valley of hunting shadows. Logan moved first.

"All right."

"You call it," Brad Quade added. He jerked Dean along and in a second again had a raving, fighting madman in his hold.

Najar struck, a Commando in-fighting blow, and the tech went limp. On the board that pulsing light was now an angry purple. And more bulbs glowed here and there, taking on a winking life. The yellow of the lightning tree was bubbling, frothing.

They crowded together on the dais, the unconscious Dean held upright between Quade and Najar. Hosteen strove to raise his hands to give the signal that would transport them out of there—and found his right arm stiff, pain holding it in a steel band to his side.

The hum of the running machines, which had always formed a purring undercurrent of sound in the hall, was a hum no longer. More of them must be coming alive.

"Your hands—hold them apart over that line of bulbs." Hosteen croaked out instructions to Logan. "Then bring them together in a fast clap—"

Logan's hands, tinted purple in that awesome light, came together. Then they were spinning out and out—

Before them once more was a patch of day. Hosteen was conscious of Logan's arm about him, of stumbling into the light, of the shuffle of feet behind.

Sound—it was not the rising hum of the alien machines but drums, a steady beat—beat of them in chorus. And over all lay the terrible need to be in the open.

They came out on that ledge where Hosteen had lain to watch Dean harangue the Norbie tribesmen. Hosteen pulled ahead, following Surra, for in the cat as well as in him was that bursting need to be away from the cave entrance.

There was no sun, and Hosteen, coming more to himself as he led the way downslope, saw now the clouds gathering in purple-black lines around an irregular space of sky. Had it been five months earlier or later, he would have said one of the terrible cloudbursts of the Wet Time was about to break.

Logan came to a halt. Surra was just a pace or so in advance, crouched belly to earth, her tail swishing, her head pointing at the line of Drummers.

They were there, every one of those who had followed their clan and tribal chieftains into the Blue—strung out in a curving line facing upslope, equidistant from each other, and each pounding out that emphatic beat that was one in a queer way with the billowing clouds. Directly before the party from the cave was Ukurti. And drawn up several yards behind the medicine men were the warriors, serried ranks of them, with here and there a truce pole still showing.

Quade and Najar, with Dean held between them, then

Hosteen and Logan—five off-world men facing a thousand or more Norbies. Had the natives come to rescue their Lord of Thunder from the impious? Logan, still propping up Hosteen, brought his other hand before him and moved fingers in the peace sign.

Not an eye blinked nor did a hand lose a fraction of the beat. Seconds became the longest minute Hosteen could remember, while that roll of sound deadened his thinking. Quade and Najar dropped their hold on Dean as if hypnotized. The tech took one stiff step forward, then another. With a set expression on his face, he was heading for Ukurti. Hosteen strove to make some move to stop the other and found that it was impossible.

But Dean had come to a halt once more. He spoke—but the sounds from his lips this time were not the trilling Norbie speech.

"Go—go—" One hand went to his throat, fingers rubbing skin, seeking the band he was not wearing now.

Ukurti's hand on an upswing remained in the air, though his fellows continued to drum. He signed slowly, and Logan, Quade, and Hosteen read his message aloud, though why they did so was beyond their comprehension.

"We-Who-Can-Drum-Thunder under the power have drummed so—and thunder will answer, as will the fire from the sky. Stop this with your own power if you can, Lord of False Lightning."

There was no mistaking the challenge delivered, not as a matter of defiance but as a pronouncement of a judge in court.

The purple-black of the clouds spread, eating up the sky, and now there were flashes of light along the circumference. Dean swayed back and forth, his fingers still rubbing frantically at his throat.

Magic—yes, this was magic of a sort, magic such as the Old Ones of Hosteen's own people had believed in and sought to use. He shook free of Logan, a racing excitement filling him. He forgot the pain of his hurt and could have shouted aloud in a feeling of triumph.

Save for the flashes of true lightning, it was night-dark. And always the drums continued to summon the storm with their power. A weird blue glow crept along rocky outcrops and made candles at the tips of tree and bush branches.

Then—just as Dean had lashed his machine-born lightning about the mountain, using it as a warning and a weapon—so did the real storm-based fire strike square behind them on the very crest of the peak. The answering shock was that of an earthquake, part of the violence young worlds knew before man arose to walk their lands.

Hosteen raised himself from the ground. He was deaf, blind, aware that some giant blow had struck close. And about him was the smell of ozone, the crisp of vegetation changed in an instant into ash.

The black of the storm clouds faded to gray. How long had he lain there? Beside him Logan stirred and sat up. Quade moved toward them on hands and knees. Najar lay where he was, moaning softly.

Downslope lay a form that did not move, and over that loomed a cloaked Drummer—Ukurti. The Norbie's head was lifted. He regarded the four men levelly, and then his hand was raised, his long forefinger pointed up and away behind them. Almost as one they shifted about to see.

Where the ledge of the cave had been was a mass of

223

rock scored and fire-blackened. And the mountain top had an odd, crumpled appearance.

Ukurti's fingers spoke. "The power has decided—Drum power against that of the hidden ancient ones. As the power has wrought, so let it be."

He turned to walk down into the valley, and before him the wave of Norbie clansmen receded. Najar got to his feet and stumbled down to view the body.

"Dean's dead—looks like the lightning got him."

"So be it," Quade said slowly, and he spoke for them all. "As Ukurti says, some power has spoken. The Lord of Thunder is dead. And this is no place for us—"

The mountain was now sealed again. Would the off-world authorities seek to reopen it for its secrets, wondered Hosteen as Quade steered him down the valley. Somehow he thought it would be a long time, if ever, before any man would tempt the retribution of the lightning power again. The "brains" might have some fancy explanation for what had happened—such as that some process inherent in the alien machines had drawn the off-season storm. But he was one in belief with Ukurti—there were powers and powers, and sometimes such met in battle. The power he could understand best had won this time. And out of that victory could come more than one kind of good, perhaps a more permanent truce between warring tribes—even Kelson's dream of the security force of Norbies and humans working together. At least there would be no Lord of Thunder to lay his lash on Arzor—and perhaps to the stars beyond.